PRAISE FOR JO NESBØ'S

MIDNIGHT SUN

"[A] many-leveled parable of the human condition, intensified by the stark, uncompromising setting of man against nature in one of the world's most inhospitable locales." —*Pittsburgh Post-Gazette*

"As much love story as crime fiction.... Should appeal to anyone who enjoys a good story." —*Minneapolis Star Tribune*

"Nesbø's writing sports a cinematic quality.... This is a single-sitting reading experience from a writer who has honed the skills of his craft." —*The Independent* (London)

"Any book from Scandinavian noir's top living writer will be on wish lists and hold lists. Have this on hand." —*Booklist*

"[An] excellent standalone. . . . Immaculately plotted and perfectly paced, the book is also darkly funny and deadly serious. . . . It has a neatly satisfying and surprisingly moving ending."

—*Publishers Weekly*
(starred review & Publishers Weekly pick)

"Wasting not a word, Nesbø paints an indelible portrait of a criminal."   —*Kirkus Reviews*

"A good writer doesn't need a 500-page doorstop to tell a story and this stand-alone from [Nesbø] proves it. *Midnight Sun* is a perfectly polished gem that can be read in a lazy afternoon."

—*The Globe and Mail* (Toronto)

Jo Nesbø

MIDNIGHT SUN

Jo Nesbø is a musician, songwriter, economist, and author. His first crime novel featuring Harry Hole was published in Norway in 1997 and was an instant hit, winning the Glass Key Award for best Nordic crime novel. He is the author of ten Harry Hole novels; *Headhunters*; *The Son*; and several children's books. His books have been translated into forty-seven languages. In 2008, he established the Harry Hole Foundation, a charity to reduce illiteracy among children in the developing world. He lives in Oslo.

www.jonesbo.com

ALSO BY JO NESBØ

Headhunters

The Son

Blood on Snow

THE HARRY HOLE SERIES

The Bat

Cockroaches

The Redbreast

Nemesis

The Devil's Star

The Redeemer

The Snowman

The Leopard

Phantom

Police

MIDNIGHT
SUN

JO NESBØ

Vintage Crime/Black Lizard

Vintage Books

A Division of Penguin Random House LLC · New York

FIRST VINTAGE CRIME/BLACK LIZARD EDITION, JANUARY 2016

English translation copyright © 2015 by Neil Smith

All rights reserved. Published in the United States by Vintage Books,
a division of Penguin Random House LLC, New York. Originally
published in Norway as *Mere Blod* by H. Aschehough & Co.
(W. Nygaard), Oslo, 2015. Copyright © 2015 by Jo Nesbø. Published
by agreement of the Salomonsson Agency. This translation was
originally published in Great Britain by Harvill Secker, an imprint of
Vintage Books, a division of Random House Group, Ltd., London, and
subsequently in hardcover in the United States by Alfred A. Knopf, a
division of Penguin Random House LLC, New York, in 2016.

Vintage is a registered trademark and Vintage Crime/Black Lizard and
colophon are trademarks of Penguin Random House LLC.

The Cataloging-in-Publication Data is on file at the Library of Congress.

Library of Congress Control Number: 2015988029

Vintage Crime/Black Lizard Trade Paperback ISBN:
978-0-8041-7257-8
eBook ISBN: 978-0-8041-72585

Book design by Betty Lew

www.weeklylizard.com

Printed in the United States of America
10 9 8 7 6 5 4 3 2

MIDNIGHT SUN

CHAPTER 1

How are we to start this story? I wish I could say that we'll start at the beginning. But I don't know where it starts. Just like everyone else, I'm not truly aware of the *real* sequence of cause and effect in my life.

Does the story start when I realised that I was only the fourth-best soccer player in the class? When Basse, my grandfather, showed me the drawings—his own drawings—of La Sagrada Família? When I took my first drag on a cigarette and heard my first track by the Grateful Dead? When I read Kant at university and thought I understood it? When I sold my first lump of hash? Or did it start when I kissed Bobby—who's actually a girl — or the first time I saw the tiny, wrinkled creature who would end up being called Anna screaming up at me? Perhaps it was when I was sitting in the Fisherman's stinking back room and he was telling me what he wanted me to do. I don't know. We store up all sorts of stories with fabricated logic, so that life can look as though it has some meaning.

So I may as well start here, in the midst of the confusion, at a time and a place where fate seemed to be taking a short break, holding its breath. When, just for a moment, I thought I was not only on my way, but had also already arrived.

I got off the bus in the middle of the night. Screwed my eyes up against the sun. It was scouring across an island out to sea, off to the north. Red and dull. Like me. Beyond it lay yet more sea. And, beyond that, the North Pole. Perhaps this was somewhere they wouldn't find me.

I looked round. In the three other points of the compass low mountain ridges sloped down towards me. Red and green heather, rocks, a few clumps of stunted birch trees. To the east the land slid into the sea, stony and flat as a pancake, and to the southwest it was as if it had been cut with a knife at the point where the sea started. A hundred metres or so above the motionless sea a plateau of open landscape took over, stretching inland. The Finnmark plateau. The end of the line, as Grandfather used to say.

The hard-packed gravel road I stood on led to a cluster of low buildings. The only thing that stuck out was the church tower. I'd woken up in my seat on the bus just as we were passing a sign with the name "Kåsund" on it, down by the shore, near a wooden jetty. And I thought, why not? and pulled the cord above the window to illuminate the stop sign above the bus driver.

I put on the jacket of my suit, grabbed my leather case and started walking. The pistol in the jacket pocket bounced against my hip. Right on the bone— I'd always been too thin. I stopped and tugged my money belt down under my shirt so that the notes would cushion the knocks.

There wasn't a cloud in the sky, and the air was so clear that I felt I could see a very long way. As far as the eye can see, as the expression goes. They say that the Finnmark plateau is beautiful. Fucked if I know. Isn't that just the sort of thing people say about inhospitable places? Either to make themselves seem a bit tough, to lay claim to some sort of insight or superiority, the way people boast about liking incomprehensible music or unreadable literature? I'd done it myself. I used to think it might make up for at least a few of the things about me that weren't good enough. Or else it was simply meant as a consolation to the few people who had to live there: "It's *so* beautiful here." Because what was so beautiful about this flat, monotonous, bleak landscape? It's like Mars. A red desert. Uninhabitable and cruel. The perfect hiding place. Hopefully.

The branches of a clump of trees by the side of the road in front of me moved. A moment later a figure leaped across the ditch and onto the road. My hand went automatically for the pistol but I stopped it: it wasn't one of them. This character looked like a joker who'd jumped straight out of a pack of cards.

"Good evening!" he called to me.

He walked towards me with a strange, rolling gait, so bandy-legged that I could see the road stretch out towards the village between his legs. As he came closer I saw he wasn't wearing a court jester's hat on his head but a Sámi cap. Blue, red and yellow—only the bells were missing. He was wearing pale leather boots, and his blue anorak, patched with black tape, had several tears revealing yellow-coloured padding that looked more like loft insulation than feathers.

"Forgive me asking," he said. "But who are you?"

He was at least two heads shorter than I. His face was broad, his grin wide, and his eyes at something of a slant. If you piled up all the clichés people in Oslo have about what a Sámi or native Laplander looked like, you'd end up with this bloke.

"I came on the bus," I said.

"So I saw. I'm Mattis."

"Mattis," I repeated, to gain a few seconds to think about the answer to his next inevitable question.

"Who are you, then?"

"Ulf," I said. It seemed as good a name as any.

"And what are you doing in Kåsund?"

"I'm just visiting," I said, nodding towards the cluster of houses.

"Who are you visiting?"

I shrugged. "No one special."

"Are you from the Countryside Commission, or are you a preacher?"

I didn't know what people from the Countryside Commission looked like, so I shook my head and ran a hand through my long, hippy hair. Maybe I should cut it. Less eye-catching.

"Forgive me asking," he said again, "but what are you, then?"

"A hunter," I said. It might have been the mention of the Countryside Commission. And it was as much the truth as it was a lie.

"Oh? Are you going to hunt here, Ulf?"

"Looks like good hunting territory."

"Yes, but you're a week early. Hunting season doesn't start until the fifteenth of August."

"Is there a hotel here?"

The Sámi smiled broadly. He coughed and spat out

a brown lump that I hoped was chewing tobacco or something similar. It hit the ground with an audible splat.

"Lodging house?" I asked.

He shook his head.

"Camping cabin? Room to rent?" On the telephone pole behind him someone had stuck up a poster about a dance band who were going to be playing in Alta. So the city couldn't be too far away. Maybe I should have stayed on the bus until it got there.

"How about you, Mattis?" I said, slapping away a gnat that was biting my forehead. "You wouldn't happen to have a bed I could borrow tonight?"

"I burned my bed in the stove back in May. We had a cold May."

"Sofa? Mattress?"

"Mattress?" He spread his hands out towards the heather-covered plateau.

"Thanks, but I like roofs and walls. I'll have to try and find an empty dog kennel. Goodnight." I set off towards the houses.

"The only kennel you'll find in Kåsund is that one," he called out plaintively, his voice falling.

I turned round. He was pointing at the building in front of the cluster of houses.

"The church?"

He nodded.

"Is it open in the middle of the night?"

Mattis tilted his head. "Do you know why no one steals anything in Kåsund? Because there's nothing worth stealing apart from reindeer."

With a surprisingly graceful leap, the chubby little man jumped across the ditch and began to tramp through the heather in a westerly direction. My guides were the sun in the north, and the fact that churches—according to my grandfather—have their towers to the west no matter where in the world you go. I shaded my eyes and looked at the terrain ahead of him. Where the hell was he going?

Maybe it was because the sun was shining even though it was the middle of the night and everything was completely still, but there was something strangely desolate about the village. The houses looked as though they had been built in a hurry, without care or love. Not that they didn't look solid, just that they gave the impression of being a roof over someone's head rather than a home. Practical. Maintenance-free slabs to stand up to wind and weather. A few wrecked cars in gardens that weren't gardens, more fenced-off areas of heather and birch trees. Prams, but no toys. Only a few of the houses had curtains or blinds in the windows. The other naked windowpanes reflected the sun, stopping anyone looking in. Like sunglasses on someone who doesn't want to reveal too much soul.

Sure enough, the church was open, although the door was swollen, so it didn't open as readily as those of other churches I had been inside. The nave was fairly small, soberly furnished, but attractive in its simplicity. The midnight sun lit up the stained-glass windows, and above the altar Jesus hung from the customary cross in front of a triptych with the Virgin Mary in the middle and David and Goliath and the baby Jesus on either side.

I found the door to the sacristy off to one side behind the altar. I searched through the cupboards and found vestments, cleaning equipment and buckets, but no altar wine, just a couple of boxes of wafers from Olsen's bakery. I chewed my way through four or five of them, but it was like eating blotting paper; they dried out my mouth so much that in the end I had to spit them out onto the newspaper on the table. Which told me—if it was that day's edition of the *Finnmark Dagblad*—that it was 8 August 1978 and that the protests against the exploitation of the Alta River were growing, and showed me what local council leader Arnulf Olsen looked like, and said that Finnmark, as the only Norwegian district that shared a border with the Soviet Union, felt a little safer now that the spy Gunvor Galtung Haavik was dead, and that at long last the weather here was better than in Oslo.

The stone floor of the sacristy was too hard to sleep on, and the pews were too narrow, so I took the vestments inside the altar rail with me, hung my jacket over the rail and lay down on the floor with my leather case under my head. I felt something wet hit my face. I wiped it away with my hand and looked at my fingertips. They were rust red.

I looked up at the crucified man hanging directly above me. Then I realised that it must have come from the pitched roof. Leaky, damp, coloured by clay or iron. I turned over so I wasn't lying on my bad shoulder and pulled the cassock over my head to shut out the sun. I closed my eyes.

There. Don't think. Shut everything out.

Shut in.

I tugged the cassock aside, gasping for breath.

Fuck.

I lay there staring at the ceiling. When I couldn't sleep after the funeral, I started taking Valium. I don't know if I got addicted to it, but it had become difficult to sleep without it. Now the only thing that worked was being sufficiently exhausted.

I pulled the cassock over me again and closed my eyes. Seventy hours on the run. One thousand, eight hundred kilometres. A couple of hours' sleep on trains and buses. I ought to be exhausted enough.

Now — happy thoughts.

I tried thinking about the way everything was before. Before before. It didn't work. Everything else popped up instead. The man dressed in white. The smell of fish. The black barrel of a pistol. Glass shattering, the fall. I thrust it aside and held out my hand, whispering her name.

And then she came at last.

I woke up. Lay perfectly still.

Something had nudged me. Someone. Gently, not so as to wake me, just to confirm that there was someone lying under the cassock.

I concentrated on breathing evenly. Maybe there was still a chance, maybe they hadn't worked out that I had woken up.

I slid my hand down to my side before remembering that I'd hung the jacket with my pistol in it on the altar rail.

Very amateurish for a professional.

CHAPTER 2

I carried on taking slow, even breaths, and felt my pulse calm down. My body had realised what my head still hadn't worked out: that if it had been them, they wouldn't have poked me, they'd just have pulled off the vestments, checked it was the right person, then peppered me worse than over-spiced mutton stew.

I carefully pulled the cassock away from my face.

The one looking down at me had freckles, a snub nose, a Band-Aid on its forehead and pale eyelashes surrounding a pair of unusually blue eyes. Topping this was a thick fringe of red hair. How old could he be? Nine? Thirteen? I had no idea, I'm hopeless at anything to do with kids.

"You can't sleep here."

I looked round. He seemed to be alone.

"Why not?" I said in a hoarse voice.

"Because Mum's got to clean there."

I got to my feet, rolled up the cassock, took my jacket from the altar rail and checked that the pistol was still in the pocket. Pain stabbed through my left shoulder as I forced it into the jacket.

"Are you from the south?" the boy asked.

"That depends what you mean by 'south.'"

"That you're from south of here, of course."

"Everyone's from south of here."

The boy tilted his head. "My name's Knut, I'm ten. What's your name?"

I was on the verge of saying something else before I remembered what I'd said the day before. "Ulf."

"How old are you, Ulf?"

"Old," I said, stretching my neck.

"More than thirty?"

The sacristy door opened. I spun round. A woman emerged, then stopped and stared at me. The first thing that struck me was that she was very young to be a cleaner. And that she looked strong. You could see the veins in her lower arm, and on the hand holding the bucket, which was overflowing with water. She had broad shoulders but a narrow waist. Her legs were hidden under an old-fashioned black pleated skirt. The other thing that struck me was her hair. It was long, and so dark that the light from the high windows made it glisten. It was held back by a simple hair clip.

She started moving again and came towards me, her shoes clattering on the floor. When she got close enough I could see that she had a fine mouth, but with a scar, perhaps from an operation to correct a harelip, on her top lip. It seemed almost unnatural, considering her dark complexion and hair, that she should have such blue eyes.

"Good morning," she said.

"Good morning. I arrived on the bus last night. And there was nowhere to . . ."

"Fine," she said. "The door here is high, and the gate is wide." She said this without warmth in her voice, put down the bucket and broom and held out her hand.

"Ulf," I said, holding out my hand to shake hers.

"The cassock," she said, waving my hand away. I looked down at the bundle in my other hand.

"I couldn't find a blanket," I said, handing her the vestments.

"And nothing to eat apart from our communion wafers," she said, unrolling and inspecting the heavy white garment.

"Sorry, of course I'll pay for—"

"You're welcome to it, with or without a blessing. But please don't spit on our council leader next time, if you don't mind."

I wasn't sure if that was a smile I could see, but the scar on her top lip seemed to twitch. Without saying anything else she turned and disappeared back into the sacristy.

I picked up my case and stepped over the altar rail.

"Where are you going?" the boy asked.

"Outside."

"What for?"

"What for? Because I don't live here."

"Mum's not as cross as she seems."

"Say goodbye from me."

"From whom?" her voice called. She was walking back towards the altar rail.

"Ulf." I was starting to get used to the name.

"And what are you doing here in Kåsund, Ulf?" She wrung out a cloth above the bucket.

"Hunting." I thought it was best to stick to one and the same story in such a small community.

She fixed the cloth to the end of the broom. "What for?"

"Grouse," I chanced. Did they have grouse this far north? "Or anything with a pulse, really," I added.

"It's been a bad year for mice and lemmings this year," she said.

I hummed. "Well, I was thinking something a *bit* bigger than that."

She raised an eyebrow. "I just meant that there aren't many grouse."

There was a pause.

In the end Knut broke it. "When predators can't get enough mice and lemmings, they take grouse eggs."

"Of course," I said with a nod, and realised my back was sweating. I could do with a wash. My shirt and money belt could do with a wash. My suit jacket could do with a wash. "I daresay I'll find something to shoot. It's more of a problem that I'm a week early. After all, hunting season doesn't start until next week. I'll just have to practise until then." I hoped the Sámi had given me accurate information.

"I don't know about a season," the woman said, pushing the broom across the floor where I had slept so hard that the broom head squeaked. "You south-erners are the ones who came up with that idea. Here we go hunting when we have to. And don't bother when there's no need."

"Speaking of needs," I said. "You don't know of anywhere in the village where I could stay?"

She stopped cleaning and leaned on the broom. "You just have to knock on a door and they'll give you a bed."

"Anywhere?"

"Yes, I'd say so. But of course there aren't that many people at home right now."

"Of course." I nodded towards Knut. "Summer holidays?"

She smiled and tilted her head. "Summer work. Anyone who's got reindeer is sleeping in tents and caravans at the pastures down by the coast. A few have gone fishing for pollock. And a lot of people have gone off to the fair in Kautokeino."

"I see. Any chance I could rent a bed from you?" When she hesitated I quickly added: "I'll pay well. Very well."

"No one here would let you pay much. But my husband isn't at home, so it's really not befitting."

Befitting? I looked at her skirt. Her long hair.

"I see. Is there anywhere that isn't so ... er, central? Where you can get some peace and quiet. With a view." By which I meant, where you can see if anyone's coming.

"Well," she said. "Seeing as you're going to be hunting, I suppose you could always stay in the hunting cabin. Everyone uses it. It's fairly remote, and a bit cramped and ramshackle, but you'd certainly get your peace and quiet. And a fine view in all directions, that much is certain."

"Sounds perfect."

"Knut can show you the way."

"There's no need for him to do that. I'm sure I can—"

"No!" Knut said. "Please!"

I looked down at him again. Summer holidays. Everyone away. Bored having to follow his mum to do her cleaning. Finally, something happening.

"Sure," I said. "Shall we go, then?"

"Yes!"

"What's bothering me," the dark-haired woman said, dipping the broom in the bucket, "is what you're going to shoot with. You've hardly got a shotgun in that case."

I stared down at my case. As if I were measuring it to see if I agreed with her.

"I left it on the train," I said. "I called them, they've promised to send it on the bus in a couple of days."

"But you'll be wanting something to practise with," she said, then smiled. "Before the *season* starts."

"I . . ."

"You can borrow my husband's shotgun. The two of you can wait outside until I'm done, this won't take long."

A shotgun? Hell, why not? And because none of her questions was phrased as a question, I simply nodded and walked towards the door. I heard quick breathing behind me and slowed down slightly. The young lad tripped over my heels.

"Ulf?"

"Yes."

"Do you know any jokes?"

I sat on the south side of the church and smoked a cigarette. I don't know why I smoke. Because I'm not addicted. I mean, my blood doesn't thirst for nicotine. It's not that. It's something else. Something to do with the act itself. It calms me down. I might as well smoke bits of straw. Am I addicted to nicotine? No, I'm sure I'm not. I might possibly be an alcoholic, but I'm really not sure about that either. But I like being high, wired, drunk, that much is obvious. I liked Valium a lot. Or rather, I really didn't like not taking Valium. That's why it was the only drug I've ever felt I had to actively cut out.

When I started dealing hash it was mainly to finance my own use. It was simple and logical: you buy enough grammes so you can haggle about the price, sell two-thirds of it in small quantities at a higher price, and hey presto, you get free dope. The path from there to turning it into a full-time occupation isn't a long one. It was the path to my first sale that was long. Long, complicated, and with a couple of twists and turns I could have done without. But there I stood, in Slott-sparken, muttering my concise sales pitch ("Dope?") to passers-by I thought had long enough hair or freaky enough clothes. And like most things in life, the first time is always the worst. So when a bloke with a crew cut and a blue shirt stopped and asked for two grammes, I freaked out and ran.

I knew he wasn't an undercover cop—they were the ones with the longest hair and the freakiest clothes. I was scared he was one of the Fisherman's men. But gradually I realised that the Fisherman didn't care about small fry like me. You just had to make sure you didn't get too big. And didn't venture into his amphet-amine and heroin market. Unlike Hoffmann. Things had ended badly for Hoffmann. There no longer was a Hoffmann.

I flicked the cigarette butt in amongst the grave-stones in front of me.

You have an allotted time, you burn down to the filter, and then it's over, for good. But the point is to burn down to the filter, and not go out before that. Well, maybe that isn't the whole point, but just then it was my goal. I don't really give a shit about the point of it. And there'd been plenty of days since the funeral when I hadn't been very sure of the goal either.

I shut my eyes and concentrated on the sun, and on feeling it warm my skin. On pleasure. Hedon. The Greek god. Or idol, as he should probably be called seeing as I was on hallowed ground. It's pretty arrogant, calling all other gods, apart from the one you've come up with, idols. *Thou shalt have no other gods before me.* Every dictator's command to his subjects, of course. The funny thing was that Christians couldn't see it themselves. They didn't see the mechanism, the regenerative, self-fulfilling, self-aggrandising aspect which meant that a superstition like this could survive for two thousand years, and in which the key—salvation—was restricted to those who were fortunate enough to have been born in a space of time which was a merest blink of the eye in human history, and who also happened to live on the only little bit of the planet that ever got to hear the commandment and were able to formulate an opinion about the concise sales pitch ("Paradise?").

The heat disappeared. A cloud was passing in front of the sun.

"That's Grandma."

I opened my eyes. It wasn't a cloud. The sun was forming a halo around the young boy's red hair. Was the woman in there really his grandmother?

"Sorry?"

He pointed. "The grave you just threw your cigarette at."

I looked past him. I could see a plume of smoke rise from the flower bed in front of a black stone. "I'm sorry. I was aiming at the path."

He folded his arms. "Really? So how are you going to hit grouse when you can't even hit a path?"

"Good question."

"Have you thought of any jokes, then?"

"No, I said it was going to take me a while."

"It's been"—he looked at the watch he didn't have—"twenty-five minutes."

It hadn't. It was beginning to dawn on me that the walk to the hunting cabin was going to be a long one.

"Knut! Leave the man alone." It was his mother. She came out through the church door and walked towards the gate.

I stood up and followed her. She had a quick stride and a way of moving that reminded me of a swan. The gravel road that went past the church led down into the cluster of houses that made up Kåsund. The stillness was almost unsettling. As yet I hadn't seen anyone else apart from these two and the Sámi last night.

"Why don't most of the houses have curtains?" I asked.

"Because Læstadius taught us to let the light of God in," she said.

"Læstadius?"

"Lars Levi Læstadius. You don't know of his teachings?"

I shook my head. I guess I'd read about the Swedish priest from the last century, who'd had to clean up the licentious ways of the locals, but I couldn't claim to know of his teachings, and I suppose I'd imagined that old-fashioned stuff like that had died out.

"Aren't you a Læstadian?" the boy asked. "You'll burn in hell, then."

"Knut!"

"But that's what Grandpa says! And he knows, because he's a travelling preacher all over Finnmark and Nord-Troms, so there!"

"Grandpa also says that you shouldn't shout your faith from the street corner." She looked at me with a pained expression. "Knut sometimes gets a bit over-zealous. Are you from Oslo?"

"Born and raised."

"Family?"

I shook my head.

"Sure?"

"What?"

She smiled. "You hesitated. Divorced, perhaps?"

"Then you'll definitely burn!" Knut cried, wiggling his fingers in a way I assumed was supposed to represent flames.

"Not divorced," I said.

I noticed her giving me a sideways look. "A lonely hunter far from home, then. What do you do otherwise?"

"Fixer," I said. A movement made me look up, and I caught a glimpse of a face behind a window before the curtain was closed again. "But I've just resigned. I'm going to try to find something new."

"Something new," she repeated. It sounded like a sigh.

"And you're a cleaner?" I asked, mostly for the sake of saying something.

"Mum's the sexton too, and the verger," Knut said. "Grandpa says she could have taken over as vicar as well. If she was a man, I mean."

"I thought they'd passed legislation about female vicars?"

She laughed. "A female vicar in Kåsund?"

The boy waggled his fingers again.

"Here we are." She turned off towards a small, curtainless house. In the drive, perched on breeze blocks, was a Volvo with no wheels, and next to it stood a wheelbarrow containing two rusty wheel rims.

"That's Dad's car," Knut said. "That one's Mum's." He pointed to a Volkswagen Beetle parked in the shade inside the garage.

We went in the unlocked house, and she showed me into the living room and said she'd fetch the shotgun, leaving me standing there with Knut. The room was sparsely furnished, neat, clean and tidy. Sturdy furniture, but no television or stereo. No potted plants. And the only pictures on the wall were Jesus carrying a sheep, and a wedding photograph.

I went closer. It was her, no doubt about that. She looked sweet, almost beautiful in her bridal gown. The man next to her was tall and broad-shouldered. For some reason, his smiling yet impassive face made me think of the face I had just caught a glimpse of in the window.

"Come here, Ulf!"

I followed the voice, through a passageway and in through the open door of what looked like a workroom. His workroom. A carpenter's bench with rusty car parts, broken children's toys that looked as though they'd been there for a while, plus several other half-finished projects.

She had pulled out a box of cartridges and pointed at a shotgun that was hanging next to a rifle balanced on two nails on the wall, too high for her to reach. I suspected she had asked me to wait in the living room so she could clear some things away in there first. I looked round for bottles, and I couldn't miss the smell of home brew, alcohol and cigarettes.

"Have you got bullets for that rifle?" I asked.

"Of course," she said. "But weren't you going to be hunting grouse?"

"It's more of a challenge with a rifle," I said, as I reached up and took it down. I aimed it out of the window. The curtains in the next house twitched. "And then you don't have the job of getting all the shot out. How do you load it?"

She looked at me intently, evidently not sure if I was joking, before she showed me. Given my job, you'd think I'd know a lot about guns, but all I know is a bit about pistols. She inserted a magazine, demonstrated the loading action, and explained that the rifle was semi-automatic, but that the hunting laws said it was illegal to have more than three bullets in the magazine and one in the chamber.

"Of course," I said, practising the loading action. What I like about guns is the sound of greased metal, of precision engineering. But that's all.

"You'll find these useful as well," she said.

I turned round. She was holding a pair of binoculars out to me. They were Soviet B8 military binoculars. My grandfather had managed to get hold of a pair somehow, which he used to study the details of church architecture. He had told me that before and during the war, all the good optical engineering came from Germany, and the first thing the Russians did when they occupied the east of the country was steal the Germans' industrial secrets and make cheaper, but damn good copies. God knows how they'd got hold of a pair of B8 binoculars here. I put the rifle down and looked through them. At the house with the face. No one there now.

"Obviously I'll pay to hire them."

"Nonsense." She replaced the box of bullets in front of me with one of rifle cartridges. "But Hugo would probably like it if you could cover the cost of the ammunition you use."

"Where is he?"

It was clearly an inappropriate question, because I saw her face twitch.

"Fishing for pollock. Have you got any food and drink?" she asked.

I shook my head. I hadn't really thought about that. How many meals had I actually eaten since Oslo?

"I'll put together some food for you, and you can get the rest from Pirjo's shop. Knut will show you."

We went back out onto the steps. She looked at the time. Presumably making sure I hadn't been inside long enough to give the neighbours anything to talk about. Knut was racing about the garden, eager as a puppy to get going.

"It'll take between thirty minutes and an hour to get to the cabin," she said. "Depending on how quick you are on your feet."

"Hmm. I'm not sure when my own shotgun's going to arrive."

"There's no rush. Hugo doesn't hunt much."

I nodded, then adjusted the strap on the rifle and slung it over my shoulder. My good shoulder. Time to get going. I tried to think of something to say in farewell. She tilted her head slightly, just like her son, and brushed some strands of hair from her face.

"You don't think it's that beautiful, do you?"

I must have looked a bit confused, because she let out a short laugh and her high cheekbones flushed. "Kåsund, I mean. Our houses. It used to be nice here. Before the war. But when the Russians came in 1945 and the Germans fled, they burned down everything that was left as they retreated. Everything except the church."

"The scorched-earth tactics."

"People needed houses. So they built quickly. With no thought to what they looked like."

"Oh, they're not *that* bad," I lied.

"Yes, they are," she laughed. "The houses are ugly. But not the people who live in them."

I looked at her scar. "I believe you. Right, time to get going. Thank you." I held out my hand. This time she took it. Her hand was firm and warm, like a smooth, sun-warmed stone.

"The peace of God."

I stared at her. She looked as if she meant it.

Pirjo's shop was in the basement of one of the houses. It was dark inside, and she only showed up after Knut had called her name three times. She was big and round, and was wearing a headscarf. She had a squeaky voice:

"*Jumalan terve.*"

"Sorry?" I said.

She turned away from me and looked at Knut.

"The peace of God," he said. "Pirjo only speaks Finnish, but she knows the Norwegian for the things in her shop."

The goods were behind the counter, and she got them out as I listed them. Tinned reindeer meatballs. Tinned fish balls. Sausages. Cheese. Crispbread.

She evidently added them up in her head, because when I was finished she just wrote a number on a piece of paper and showed it to me. I realised that I should have taken some notes out of the money belt before I went in. Seeing as I didn't want to advertise the fact that I was carrying a serious amount of money, around a hundred and thirteen thousand kroner, I turned my back on the other two and undid the bottom two buttons of my shirt.

"You're not allowed to pee in here, Ulf," Knut said.

I half-turned to look at him.

"I was joking," he said with a laugh.

Pirjo gestured that she couldn't change the hundred-kroner note I gave her.

"Don't worry," I said. "Take it as a tip."

She said something in her harsh, incomprehensible language.

"She says you can have more supplies when you come back," Knut said.

"Maybe she should write the outstanding amount down."

"She'll remember," Knut said. "Come on."

Knut danced ahead of me on the path. The heather brushed my trouser legs and the midges buzzed around our heads. The plateau.

"Ulf?"

"Yes?"

"Why have you got such long hair?"

"Because no one's cut it."

"Oh."

Twenty seconds later.

"Ulf?"

"Hmm?"

"Do you know *any* Finnish?"

"No."

"Sámi?"

"Not a word."

"Just Norwegian?"

"And English."

"Are there lots of English people down in Oslo?"

I squinted at the sun. If it was the middle of the day, that meant we were walking more or less directly west. "Not really," I said. "But it's a global language."

"A global language, yes. That's what Grandpa says too. He says Norwegian is the language of common sense. But Sámi is the language of the heart. And Finnish is the holy language."

"If he says so."

"Ulf?"

"Yes?"

"I know a joke."

"Okay."

He stopped and waited for me to catch up, then set off beside me through the heather. "What keeps going but never reaches the door?"

"That's a riddle, isn't it?"

"Shall I tell you the answer?"

"Yes, I think you're going to have to."

He shaded his eyes with his hand and grinned up at me. "You're lying, Ulf."

"Sorry?"

"You know the answer!"

"Do I?"

"Everyone knows the answer to that riddle. Why do you all keep lying? You'll end up—"

"Burning in hell?"

"Yes!"

"Who are 'you all'?"

"Dad. And Uncle Ove. And Mum."

"Really? What does your mum lie about?"

"She says there's no need for me to worry about Dad. Now it's your turn to tell a joke."

"I'm not much good at telling jokes."

He stopped and leaned forward, with his arms dangling towards the heather. "You can't hit a target, you don't know anything about grouse, and you can't tell jokes. Is there anything you *can* do?"

"Oh, yes," I said, as I watched a solitary bird drift on its wings high above us. Watching. Hunting. Something about its stiff, angled wings made me think of a warplane. "I can hide."

"Yes!" His head shot up. "Let's play hide-and-seek! Who's going to start? Eeny, meeny, miny, mo . . ."

"You run ahead and hide."

He ran three paces and then stopped abruptly.

"What is it?"

"You're only saying that because you want to get rid of me."

"Get rid of you? Never!"

"Now you're lying again!"

I shrugged. "We can play the being-quiet game. Anyone who isn't completely quiet gets shot in the head."

He gave me a funny look.

"Not for real," I said. "Okay?"

He nodded, his mouth tight shut.

"From now," I said.

We walked and walked. The scenery which had looked so monotonous from a distance was constantly changing, from soft, earthy browns covered by green and reddish-brown heather, to stony, scarred lunar landscapes, and suddenly—in the light of the sun which had turned half a revolution since I arrived, like a golden red discus—it looked like it was glowing, as though lava were running down the gently sloping hillsides. Above it all was a vast, broad sky. I don't know why it seemed so much bigger here, or why I imagined I could see the curvature of the earth. Maybe it was lack of sleep. I've read that people can become psychotic after just two days without sleep.

Knut marched on in silence, with a determined look on his freckled face. There were more clouds of midges now, until eventually they formed one great big swarm that we couldn't escape. I'd stopped swatting them when they landed on me. They punctured my skin with their anaesthetised bites, and the whole business was so gentle that I left them to it. The important thing was that I was putting metre after metre—kilometres—between me and civilisation. Even so, I needed to come up with a plan soon.

The Fisherman always finds what he's looking for.

The plan up to now had been not to have a plan, seeing as he would be able to predict every logical plan I could come up with. My only chance was unpredictability. Acting so erratically that even I didn't know what my next move was going to be. But I'd have to think of something after that. If there was any "after that."

"A clock," Knut said. "The answer's a clock."

I nodded. It was only a matter of time.

"And now you can shoot me in the head, Ulf."

"Okay."

"Go on, then!"

"What for?"

"To get it over with. There's nothing worse than not knowing when the bullet's coming."

"Bang."

"Did you get teased at school, Ulf?"

"Why do you ask?"

"You've got a weird way of talking."

"Everyone talks like this where I grew up."

"Wow. Did they all get teased, then?"

I couldn't help laughing. "Okay, I got teased a *bit*. When I was ten years old my parents died, and I moved from the east side of Oslo to the west, to live with my grandfather, Basse. The other kids called me Oliver Twist and east-end trash."

"But you're not."

"Thanks."

"You're south-side trash." He laughed. "That was a joke! That's three you owe me now."

"I wish I knew where you got them all from, Knut."

He screwed one eye shut and squinted at me. "Can I carry the rifle?"

"No."

"It's my dad's."

"I said no."

He groaned, and drooped his head and arms for a few seconds, then straightened again. We sped up. He sang quietly to himself. I couldn't swear to it, but it sounded like a hymn. I thought about asking him what his mother's name was—it might be useful to know when I needed to go back to the village. If I couldn't remember where the house was, for instance. But for some reason I couldn't bring myself to ask.

"There's the cabin," Knut said, and pointed.

I got the binoculars out and adjusted the focus, which you have to do with both lenses on a B8. Behind the dancing midges lay something that looked more like a small woodshed than a cabin. No windows, from what I could see, just a collection of unpainted, grey, dried-out planks gathered around a thin, black chimney pipe.

We carried on walking, and my mind must have been on something else entirely when my eyes registered a movement, something much bigger than the midges, something a hundred metres ahead of us, something suddenly emerging from the monotonous landscape. My heart felt as though it stopped for a moment. There was an odd clicking sound as the heavy-antlered creature ran off through the heather.

"A buck," Knut declared.

My pulse slowly calmed down. "How do you know it's not a . . . er, one of the other sort?"

He gave me that funny look again.

"We don't get many reindeer in Oslo," I said.

"A doe. Because bucks have bigger horns, don't they? See, it's rubbing them against that tree."

The reindeer had stopped in a cluster of trees behind the cabin and was rubbing its antlers against a birch trunk.

"Is it scraping off bark to eat?"

He laughed. "Reindeer eat lichen."

Of course, reindeer eat lichen. We'd learned about the types of moss that grow up here close to the North Pole in school. That a *joik* was a sort of improvised shouting in Sámi, that a *lavvo* was a form of Indian tepee, and that Finnmark was further away from Oslo than London or Paris. We also learned a way of remembering the names of the fjords, although I doubt anyone could recall what it was now. Not me, anyway—I'd made it through fifteen years of education, two of them at university, even, by half-remembering things.

"They rub their horns to clean them," Knut said. "They do that in August. When I was little, Grandpa said it was because their horns itched so badly."

He smacked his lips like an old man, as if to lament how naive he had once been. I could have told him that some of us never stop being naive.

The cabin stood on four large rocks. It wasn't locked, but I had to tug the door handle hard to loosen it from the frame. Inside were a pair of bunk beds with woollen blankets, and a wood-burning stove with a dented kettle and a casserole dish sitting on its two hotplates. There was an orange wall cupboard, a red plastic bucket, two chairs and a table that leaned towards the west, either because it was crooked or because the floor was uneven.

The cabin did have windows. The reason I hadn't seen them was that they were just embrasures, narrow slits in all the walls except for the one with the door in it. But they let in enough light, and you could see anything approaching from every direction. Even when I walked the three steps from one end of the cabin to the other and felt the whole building wobble like a French coffee table, it didn't change my initial conclusion: the cabin was perfect.

I looked round and thought of the first thing Grandfather said when he had carried my trunk up to his house and unlocked it: *Mi casa es tu casa.* And even though I didn't understand a word, I still guessed what it meant.

"Do you want coffee before you walk back?" I asked nonchalantly as I opened the wood-burning stove. Fine grey ash blew out.

"I'm ten years old," Knut said. "I don't drink coffee. You need wood. And water."

"So I see. A slice of bread, then?"

"Have you got an axe? Or a knife?"

I looked at him without replying. He looked up at the ceiling in response. A hunter with no knife.

"You can borrow this for the time being," Knut said, reaching behind his back and pulling out an enormous knife with a broad blade and a yellow wooden handle.

I turned the knife in my hand. Heavy, but not too heavy, and nicely balanced. Pretty much the way a pistol should feel.

"Did you get this from your dad?"

"From Grandpa. It's a Sámi knife."

We agreed that he would gather wood while I fetched water. He evidently liked being given a grown-up task, and grabbed the knife back and ran out. I found a loose plank in the wall. Behind it, between the two walls, was a sort of insulation made of moss and turf, and I pushed the money belt into that. I could hear the sound of steel against wood from the clump of trees as I filled the plastic bucket in the stream that ran just a hundred metres from the cabin.

Knut put some kindling and bark in the stove while I cleared the mouse shit from the cupboard and put the food away. I lent him my matches and before long the stove was alight and the kettle was hissing. Some smoke leaked out, and I noticed that the midges were holding back. I took the opportunity to take my shirt off and splash some water from the bucket on my face and upper body.

"What's that?" Knut asked, pointing.

"This?" I said, taking hold of the dog tag hanging round my neck. "Name and date of birth engraved on bombproof metal, so they know who they've killed."

"Why would they want to know that?"

"So they know where to send the skeleton."

"Ha, ha," he said drily. "*Doesn't* count as a joke."

The hissing of the kettle was replaced by a warning rumble. As I filled one of the two chipped coffee cups, Knut was already halfway through his second thick slice of bread with liver pâté. I blew on the black, greasy surface of the coffee.

"What does coffee taste like?" Knut asked with his mouth full.

"The first time's always the worst," I said, and took a sip. "Eat up, then you'd better get going before your mum wonders where you are."

"She knows where I am." He put both elbows on the table and leaned his head on his hands, pushing his cheeks up over his eyes. "Joke."

The coffee tasted perfect, and the cup warmed my hands. "Have you heard the one about the Norwegian, the Dane and the Swede, who had a bet to see who could lean farthest out of the window?"

He took his arms off the table and stared at me expectantly. "No."

"They were sitting on the windowsill. And suddenly the Norwegian won."

In the silence that followed I took another sip. I assumed from Knut's gawping expression that he hadn't figured out that was the end of the joke.

"How did he win?" he asked.

"How do you think? The Norwegian fell out of the window."

"So the Norwegian bet on himself?"

"Obviously."

"*Not* obviously. You should have said that from the start."

"Okay, but you get the point." I sighed. "So what do you think?"

He put one finger under his freckled chin and stared thoughtfully into space. Then came two loud bursts of laughter. Then more thoughtful staring.

"A bit short," he said. "But that's probably what makes it funny. Bang—it's all over. Well, it made me laugh." He laughed a bit more.

"Speaking of things being over . . ."

"Of course," he said, standing up. "I'll come back tomorrow."

"Really? Why?"

"Midge oil."

"Midge oil?"

He took my hand and put it to my forehead. It was like bubble wrap, bump upon bump.

"Okay," I said. "Bring midge oil. And beer."

"Beer? Then you'll—"

"Burn in hell?"

"Have to go to Alta."

I thought about the smell in his father's workroom. "Hooch."

"Huh?"

"Home brew. Moonshine. Whatever your father drinks. Where does he get it from?"

Knut shifted his weight a couple of times. "Mattis."

"Hmm. Bow-legged little fellow in a torn anorak?"

"Yes."

I took a note out of my pocket. "See how much you can get with this, and get yourself an ice cream. Unless that's a sin, of course."

He shook his head and took the note. "Goodbye, Ulf. And keep the door closed."

"Oh, there probably isn't room for any more midges in here."

"Not midges. Wolves."

Was he kidding?

When he had gone I picked up the rifle and rested it on one of the sills. I looked through the sights as I swept the horizon. I found Knut as he skipped away down the path. I carried on towards the little patch of woodland. I found the buck. At that moment it raised its head, as if it could sense me. As far as I knew, reindeer were herd animals, so this one must have been expelled. Like me.

I went and sat down outside the cabin and drank the rest of the coffee. The heat and the smoke from the stove had given me a thumping headache.

I looked at the time. Almost one hundred hours had passed now. Since I should have died. One hundred bonus hours.

When I looked out again the buck had come closer.

CHAPTER 3

One hundred hours ago.

But it had started long before that. Like I said, I don't know how. Let's say it started a year earlier, the day Brynhildsen came over to me in Slottsparken. I was stressed out: I'd only just discovered she was ill.

Brynhildsen had a hook nose and a pencil moustache, and had lost his hair early. He had worked for Hoffmann before the Fisherman inherited him, along with the rest of Hoffmann's estate—in other words, his share of the heroin market, his woman, and a big apartment on Bygdøy allé. Brynhildsen said the Fisherman wanted to talk to me, and that I should report to the fish shop. Then he walked away.

Grandfather was very fond of the Spanish proverbs he had picked up when he lived in Barcelona, drawing his version of La Sagrada Família. One of the ones I heard most often was: "There weren't many of us in the house, and then Grandma got pregnant." It meant something along the lines of: "As if we didn't already have enough problems."

All the same, I turned up at the Fisherman's shop on Youngstorget the next day. Not because I wanted to, but because the alternative—not turning up—was out of the question. The Fisherman was too powerful. Too dangerous. Everyone knew the story of how he had cut Hoffmann's head off, saying that was what happened when you got ideas above your station. Or the story of two of his dealers who suddenly disappeared after helping themselves to a share of the goods. No one ever saw them again. There were those who claimed the fish balls from his shop had been extra tasty in the following few months. He did nothing to stop the rumours. That's how a businessman like the Fisherman defends his territory, with a mixture of rumour, half-truths and hard facts about what happens to people who try to trick him.

I hadn't tried to trick the Fisherman. Even so, I was sweating like a junkie going cold turkey as I stood in his shop and told one of the older women behind the counter who I was. I don't know if she pressed a buzzer or something, but the Fisherman came out through the swing door behind them immediately afterwards, with a broad smile, dressed from head to toe in white—a white cap, white shirt and apron, white trousers, white wooden shoes—and extended his big, wet hand to me.

We went into the back room. White tiles on the floor and all the walls. The benches along the walls were covered with metal dishes containing corpse-pale fillets marinating in brine.

"Sorry about the smell, Jon, I'm making fish balls." The Fisherman pulled out a chair from under the metal table in the middle of the room. "Sit down."

"I only sell hash," I said, as I did what he told me. "Never speed or heroin."

"I know. The reason I wanted to talk to you is that you killed one of my employees. Toralf Jonsen."

I stared at him, speechless. I was dead. I was going to become fish balls.

"Very clever, Jon. And it was a smart move to make it look like a suicide—everyone knew Toralf could be a little . . . gloomy." The Fisherman tore off part of one fillet and popped it in his mouth. "Even the police didn't think his death was suspicious. I have to admit that I thought he'd shot himself as well. Until an acquaintance in the police quietly informed us that the pistol that was found next to him was registered in your name. Jon Hansen. So we took a closer look. That was when Toralf's girlfriend told us he owed you money. That you'd tried to get it off him a couple of days before he died. That's right, isn't it?"

I gulped. "Toralf smoked a fair bit. We knew each other well, childhood friends, shared a flat for a while, that sort of thing. So I let him have credit." I tried a smile. Then I realised how ridiculous it must have looked. "Always stupid to have different rules for friends in this game, isn't it?"

The Fisherman smiled back, suspended one fillet by a piece of sinew and studied it as it slowly turned in the air. "You should never let friends, family or employees owe you money, Jon. Never. Okay, so you let the debt stand for a while, but when it came down to it you knew that rules have to be upheld. You're like me, Jon. A man of principle. Those who cross you must be punished. Doesn't matter if the transgression is big or small. Doesn't matter if it's a dropout you don't know or your own brother. That's the only way to protect your territory. Even a shitty little business like yours over in Slottsparken. How much do you earn? Five thousand a month? Six?"

I shrugged. "Something like that."

"I respect what you did."

"But—"

"Toralf was extremely important to me. He was my collector. And, if necessary, my fixer. He was willing to fix bad debtors. Not everyone's prepared to do that in today's society. People have got so soft. It's become possible to be soft yet still survive. It's"—he stuffed the whole fillet in his mouth—"perverse."

While he chewed I considered my options. Getting up and running out through the shop and into the square looked like the best of them.

"So, as you can appreciate, you've left me with something of a problem," he said.

Obviously they'd come after me and catch me, but maybe I could avoid ending up in the fish-ball mixture if they had to take me down out in the street.

"I'm thinking, who do I know who's got what it takes to do what has to be done? Who can kill? I only know two. One is efficient, but enjoys killing a bit too much, and that sort of pleasure strikes me as"—he picked at his front teeth—"perverse." He studied his fingertip. "Besides, he doesn't cut his fingernails properly. And I don't need a girlie pervert. I need someone who can talk to people. Talk first, then, if that doesn't work, fix them. So how much do you want, Jon?"

"Sorry?"

"I want to know what you'd be happy with. Eight thousand a month?"

I blinked.

"No? Shall we say ten? Plus a bonus of thirty for anyone you fix."

"Are you asking me if—?"

"Twelve. Damn, you're a tough cookie, Jon. But that's fine, I respect that as well."

I breathed hard through my nose. He was asking me to take Toralf's place as his collector and fixer.

I swallowed. And thought.

I didn't want the job.

I didn't want the money.

But I needed it.

She needed it.

"Twelve . . ." I said. "That sounds fine."

It was a simple job.

All I had to do was turn up and say I was the Fisherman's collector, and the money appeared. And I wasn't exactly overworked; I mostly sat in the back room of the shop playing cards with Brynhildsen, who always cheated, and Styrker, who never stopped talking about his damn Rottweilers and how efficient they were. I was bored, I was worried, but the money kept coming, and I had calculated that if I worked for him for at least a few months, I could pay for a year's treatment. Hopefully that would be enough. And you get used to most things, even the smell of fish.

One day the Fisherman came in and said he had a slightly bigger job that required both discretion and a firm hand.

"He's been buying speed from me for years," the Fisherman said. "Seeing as he's not a friend, a relative or an employee, I've let him have credit. It's never been a problem, but now he's fallen behind with the payments."

It was Kosmos, an older guy who sold speed from a table in the Goldfish, the grubby café down by the docks. The windows were grey from the heavy traffic that ran right past, and there were rarely more than three or four people inside.

The way Kosmos did business was as follows: the customer wanting speed came in and sat down at the next table, which was always empty because Kosmos had draped his coat over one chair and left a copy of *Hjemmet* on the table. He would be sitting at his own table doing a crossword in one of the papers. *Aftenposten* or *VG*'s mini crossword or Helge Seip's big one in *Dagbladet*. And *Hjemmet*, of course. Apparently he'd twice been crowned national crossword champion in *Hjemmet*. You slipped an envelope containing money inside the magazine and went to the toilet, and when you came back the envelope contained speed instead of cash.

It was early in the morning and, as usual, there were only three or four other customers when I arrived. I sat down two tables away from the old man, ordered a coffee and turned to the crossword. I scratched my head with my pencil. Leaned over.

"Excuse me?"

I had to repeat it twice before Kosmos looked up from his own crossword. He was wearing glasses with orange lenses.

"Sorry, but I need a four-letter word for 'outstanding.' First letter *d.*"

"Debt," he said, and looked down again.

"Of course. Thanks." I filled in the letters.

I waited a while, took a sip of the weak coffee. Cleared my throat: "Excuse me, I shan't keep pestering you, but could you help me with 'trawlerman,' nine letters? The first two letters are *f* and *i.*"

"Fisherman," he said without looking up. But I saw him start as he heard himself say the word.

"One last word," I said. "Six letters, 'tool,' starts with an *h.* Two *m*'s in the middle."

He pushed the newspaper away and looked at me. His Adam's apple was bobbing up and down on his unshaven neck.

I smiled apologetically. "I'm afraid the deadline for the crossword expires this afternoon. I've got to go off and sort something out, but I'll be back in exactly two hours' time. I'll leave the paper here so you can fill in the answers, if you can sort it out."

I went down to the harbour, smoked a bit and did some thinking. I didn't know what was going on, why he hadn't managed to pay off the debt. And I didn't want to know either. I didn't want his desperate face fixed on my retina. Not another one. The pale little face on the pillow bearing the washed-out logo of Ullevål Hospital was enough.

When I got back Kosmos looked absorbed in his crossword, but when I opened my newspaper there was an envelope there.

The Fisherman later told me he'd paid in full, and said I was good at my job. But what help was that? I'd talked to the doctors. The prognosis wasn't good. She wouldn't see out the year if she didn't get treatment. So I went to the Fisherman and explained the situation. Said I needed a loan.

"Sorry, Jon, no can do. You're an employee, aren't you?"

I nodded. What the hell was I going to do?

"But maybe we've got a solution to your problem after all. I need someone fixed."

Oh, shit.

It had to happen sooner or later, but I'd been hoping for later. After I'd saved up what I needed and handed in my notice.

"I heard your favourite expression is that the first time is always the worst," he said. "So you're lucky. That it isn't the first time, I mean."

I tried to smile. He couldn't know, after all. That I hadn't killed Toralf. That the pistol registered in my name was a small-calibre thing from a sports club that Toralf needed for a job, but hadn't been able to buy for himself because he had a record as an East German dissenter. So I—who'd never been arrested, not for my little hash business or anything else—had bought it for him in return for a small fee. I hadn't seen it since. And I'd given up on the money I'd tried to get back because she needed it for treatment. Toralf, the depressed, drugged-up bastard, had done exactly what it looked like he'd done: he'd shot himself.

I had no principles. No money. But neither did I have blood on my hands.

Not yet.

A bonus of thirty thousand.

That was a start. A good start.

I jerked awake. The midge bites were weeping and sticking to the wool blanket. But that wasn't what had woken me. A plaintive howl had broken the silence out on the plateau.

A wolf? I thought they howled at the moon, in winter, not at the fucking sun that just hung there in the burned-out, colourless sky. It was probably a dog: the Sámi used them to herd reindeer, didn't they?

I rolled over in the narrow bunk, forgetting my bad shoulder, swore, and rolled back. The howl sounded as though it was a long way away, but who knows? In the summer sound is supposed to move more slowly, doesn't carry as far as it does in winter. Maybe the beast was just round the corner.

I closed my eyes, but knew I wasn't going to get back to sleep.

So I got up, grabbed the binoculars and went over to one of the windows and scanned the horizon.

Nothing.

Just tick-tock, tick-tock.

CHAPTER 4

Knut brought some shiny, sticky, stinking midge oil which could well have been napalm. Plus two unmarked bottles with cork stoppers containing a bright stinking liquid which was definitely napalm. The morning had brought no respite from the relentless sun, as well as a wind that whistled in the stovepipe. The shadows of tiny clouds slid across the desolate, monotonous, rolling landscape like herds of reindeer, momentarily colouring the pale green stretches of vegetation a darker shade, swallowing the reflections from the small pools in the distance and the shimmer of the minute crystals where the rocks lay bare. Like a sudden, deep bass note in an otherwise bright song. Either way, it was still in a minor key.

"Mum says you're very welcome to join our congregation in the prayer house," the boy said. He was sitting opposite me at the table.

"Really?" I said, running my hand over one of the bottles. I'd put the cork back in without tasting it. Foreplay. You had to drag it out, that made it even better. Or worse.

"She thinks you can be saved."

"But you don't?"

"I don't think you want to be saved."

I stood up and went over to the window. The reindeer buck was back. When I saw it earlier that morning I realised that I felt relieved. Wolves. They'd been wiped out in Norway, hadn't they?

"My grandfather drew churches," I said. "He used to be an architect. But he didn't believe in God. He said that when we died, we died. I'm more inclined to believe that."

"He didn't believe in Jesus either?"

"If he didn't believe in God, he was hardly going to believe in his son, Knut."

"I get it."

"You get it. So?"

"So he'll burn in hell."

"Hmmmm. In that case he's been burning for a

while, because he died when I was nineteen. Don't you think that's a bit unfair? Basse was a good man, he gave a helping hand to people who needed it, which is more than you can say about a lot of Christians I've known. If I could be half as good a man as my grandfather . . ."

I blinked. My eyes were stinging and I could see little white dots floating in front of them. Was all this sunlight burning holes in my retinas, was I going snow-blind now, in the middle of the summer?

"Grandpa says doing good deeds doesn't help, Ulf. Your grandfather's burning now, and soon it'll be your turn."

"Hmm. But you're saying that if I go to the meeting and say yes to Jesus and this Læstadius, I'll get to paradise even if I do nothing at all to help anyone else?"

The boy scratched his red hair. "Yeees. Well, if you say yes to the Lyngen branch."

"There's more than one branch?"

"There are the Firstborns in Alta, and the Lundbergians in South Tromsø, and the Old Læstadians in America, and—"

"And they're all going to burn?"

"Grandpa says they will."

"Sounds like there's going to be plenty of room in paradise. Have you thought about what would happen if you and I had switched grandfathers? Then you'd have been an atheist and me a Læstadian. And then you'd be the one who'd burn in hell."

"Maybe. But fortunately you're the one who's going to burn, Ulf."

I sighed. There was something so settled about the landscape here. As if nothing was going to happen, or could ever happen, as if lack of change was its natural state.

"Ulf?"

"Yes?"

"Do you miss your father?"

"No."

Knut stopped. "Wasn't he nice?"

"I think he was. But we're good at forgetting when we're children."

"Is that allowed?" he asked in a quiet voice. "Not missing your father?"

I looked at him. "I think so," I yawned. My shoulder ached. I needed a drink.

"Are you really completely alone, Ulf? Haven't you got *anyone*?"

I thought for a moment. I actually had to do that, *think* about it. Dear God.

I shook my head.

"Guess who I'm thinking about, Ulf."

"Your father and grandpa?"

"No," he said. "I'm thinking about Ristiinna."

I didn't bother asking how he thought I might be able to guess that. My tongue felt like a dried-out sponge, but that drink would have to wait until he'd finished talking and left. He'd even given me some of the money back. "So who's Ristiinna?"

"She's in year five. She's got long, golden hair. She's at summer camp in Kautokeino. We were supposed to be there too."

"What sort of camp is it?"

"Just a camp."

"And what do you do there?"

"Us kids play. When there aren't meetings and sermons, I mean. But now Roger will ask if Ristiinna wants to be his girlfriend. And they might kiss."

"Isn't kissing a sin, then?"

He tilted his head. Screwed one eye up. "I don't know. Before she left I told her I loved her."

"You said you loved her, straight out?"

"Yes." He leaned forward and said in a breathy voice with a faraway look in his eyes: *"I love you, Ristiinna."* Then he looked up at me again. "Was that wrong?"

I smiled. "Not really. What did she say?"

"Okay."

"She said 'okay'?"

"Yes. What do you think that means, Ulf?"

"Well, who knows? Obviously it might mean that

it was all a bit much for her. 'Love' is a pretty big word. But it might mean that she wants to think about it."

"Do you think I have a chance?"

"Definitely."

"Even if I've got a scar?"

"What scar?"

He lifted the Band-Aid on his forehead. The pale skin underneath still showed signs of stitches.

"What happened?"

"I fell down the stairs."

"Tell her you had a fight with a buck, that you were fighting for territory. And that you won, obviously."

"Are you stupid? She won't believe that!"

"No, because it's only a joke. Girls like boys who can tell jokes."

He bit his top lip. "You're not lying, are you, Ulf?"

"Okay, listen. If it turns out that you don't have a chance with this particular Ristiinna this particular summer, there'll be other Ristiinnas and other summers. You're going to have loads of girls."

"Why?"

"Why?" I looked him up and down. Was he small for his age? He was certainly bright for someone his size. Red hair and freckles might not be a winning combination with women, but fashions like that came and went. "If you ask me, you're Finnmark's answer to Mick Jagger."

"Huh?"

"James Bond."

He looked blankly at me.

"Paul McCartney?" I tried. No reaction. "The Beatles. *She loves you, yeah, yeah, yeah.*"

"You're not very good at singing, Ulf."

"True." I opened the stove door, poked a damp cloth inside, then rubbed the moist ash on the shiny, worn sights of the rifle. "Why aren't you at summer camp?"

"Dad's fishing for pollock, we've got to wait for him."

There was something, a twitch at the corner of his mouth, something that didn't make sense. Something I decided not to ask about. I looked along the sights. With a bit of luck, now the sun wouldn't reflect off it and give away my location as I took aim at them when they came.

"Let's go outside," I said.

The wind had blown the midges away, and we sat in the sunshine. The buck moved further off when we came out. Knut had his knife with him, and sat there sharpening a stick.

"Ulf?"

"You don't have to say my name every time you want to ask something."

"Okay. But Ulf?"

"Yes?"

"Are you going to get drunk when I've gone?"

"No," I lied.

"Good."

"Are you worried about me?"

"I just think it's a bit stupid that you're going to end up—"

"Burning in hell?"

He laughed. Then held the stick up as he tried to whistle through his teeth.

"Ulf?"

I sighed wearily. "Yes?"

"Have you robbed a bank?"

"What on earth makes you think that?"

"All the money you've got on you."

I pulled out my cigarettes. Fumbled slightly with the packet. "Travelling's expensive," I said. "And I haven't got a chequebook."

"And the pistol in your jacket pocket."

I peered at him as I tried to light a cigarette, but the wind blew the flame out. So the boy had searched my jacket before he woke me in the church.

"You have to be careful when you've got cash and no chequebook."

"Ulf?"

"Yes."

"You're not very good at lying either."

I laughed. "What's that stick going to be?"

"A thole pin," he said, and carried on whittling.

It was much more peaceful once the boy had gone. Obviously. But I wouldn't have minded if he'd stayed a bit longer. Because I had to admit that he had a certain entertainment value.

I sat and dozed. I screwed up my eyes and saw that the buck had come closer again. It must have got used to me. It looked so lonely. You'd think reindeer ought to be fat at this time of year, but this one was skinny. Skinny, grey, and with pointlessly large antlers that had probably got it some females in the past, but now looked as if they were mostly just in the way.

The buck was so close that I could hear it chewing. It raised its head and looked at me. Well, towards me. Reindeer have bad eyesight. They rely on their sense of smell. It could smell me.

I shut my eyes.

How long ago was it now? Two years? One? The guy I was supposed to fix was called Gustavo, and I struck at dawn. He lived alone in a small, forsaken wooden house squeezed in between the tenement blocks of Homansbyen. Some fresh snow had fallen, but it was supposed to get milder during the day, and I remember thinking that my footprints would melt away.

I rang the doorbell, and when he opened up I held the pistol to his forehead. He backed away and I followed him. I shut the door behind us. The house smelled of smoke and cooking fat. The Fisherman had told me he'd recently found out that Gustavo, who was one of his permanent street-dealers, had been stealing money and dope. My job was to shoot him, plain and simple. And if I had done so there and then, things would have been very different. But I made two mistakes: I looked at his face. And I let him talk.

"Are you going to shoot me?"

"Yes," I said. Instead of firing. He had brown puppy-dog eyes, and a wispy moustache that drooped sadly on either side of his mouth.

"How much is the Fisherman paying you?"

"Enough." I squeezed the trigger. One of his eye-balls quivered. He yawned. I've heard that dogs yawn when they're nervous. But the trigger didn't work. Wrong, my finger didn't work. Fucking hell. In the hallway behind him I saw a shelf with a pair of mittens and a blue woollen hat on it.

"Put the hat on," I said.

"What?"

"The woolly hat. Pull it down over your face. Now. Otherwise . . ."

He did as I said. Became a soft, blue doll's head with no features. He still looked pathetic as he stood there with his little pot belly under his Esso T-shirt and his arms hanging limply by his sides. But I thought I could do this. As long as I didn't have to see his face. I took aim at the hat.

"We can share." I saw his mouth move behind the wool.

I fired. I was sure I'd fired. But I couldn't have done, because I could still hear his voice:

"If you let me go, you can have half the money and amphetamines. That's ninety thousand in cash alone. And the Fisherman will never find out, because I'll disappear for good. Go abroad, get myself a new identity. I swear."

The brain is a strange and wonderful thing. While one part of my brain knew that this was an idiotic, lethal idea, another part was thinking hard about it. Ninety thousand. Plus the bonus of thirty thousand. And I wouldn't have to shoot the guy.

"If you ever show up again, I'm finished," I said.

"We'd both be finished," he said. "You can have the money belt into the bargain."

Fuck.

"The Fisherman's expecting a body."

"Say you had to get rid of it."

"Why would I have to do that?"

Silence under the hat. For two seconds. "Because

it held incriminating evidence against you. You were expecting to shoot me straight through the head, but the bullet didn't come out again. That fits with the little pea-shooter you've got there. The bullet got stuck inside my head, and the bullet could link you to the murder because you used that pea-shooter in another shooting. So you had to stick my body in your car and dump it in Bunnefjorden."

"I haven't got a car."

"You took my car, then. We can leave it at Bunnefjorden. You've got a licence?"

I nodded. Then realised he couldn't see. And realised what a bad idea this was. I raised the pistol again. Too late, he'd pulled off the hat and was grinning at me. Animated eyes. A gold tooth glinted.

In hindsight it's easy to ask why I didn't just shoot Gustavo in the cellar *after* he'd given me the money and drugs that were buried in the coal bin. I could have just switched out the light and fired off a shot to the back of his head. Then the Fisherman would have had his body, I wouldn't just have half but *all* of the money, and I wouldn't have been left wondering when Gustavo was going to show up again. It should have been a simple calculation for a wonderful brain. And it was. The problem was that it was worth more to me not to have to put a bullet in his head. And I knew he was going to need half the money to get away and stay hidden. When it comes down to it, I'm just a pathetic, weak fool who deserves all the crap fate has thrown at me.

But Anna didn't deserve it.

Anna deserved better.

She deserved a chance to live.

A clicking sound.

I opened my eyes. The buck was running off.

Someone was coming.

CHAPTER 5

I saw him through the binoculars.

He had a rolling gait, and he was so short and bow-legged that the heather brushed his crotch.

I lowered the rifle.

When he reached the cabin he pulled off his joker's hat and wiped away the sweat. Grinned.

"An ice-cold *viidna* would be good right now."

"I'm afraid I haven't—"

"Sámi aquavit. Distilled by the best. You've got two bottles."

I shrugged my shoulders and we went inside. I opened one of the bottles. Poured clear, room-temperature liquid into the two cups.

"Cheers," Mattis said, raising one of them.

I said nothing, and merely gulped the poison down. He quickly followed my example. Wiped his mouth. "Ah, that was good." He held his cup out.

I filled it. "Did you follow Knut?"

"I knew the *viidna* wasn't for his father, so I had to make sure the lad wasn't thinking of drinking it himself. You have to show a bit of responsibility." He grinned, and a brown liquid dribbled down from behind his top lip and over his yellow front teeth. "So this is where you're staying."

I nodded.

"How's the hunting going?"

I shrugged. "Not many grouse about when it's been such a bad year for mice and lemmings."

"You've got a rifle. And there are plenty of wild reindeer in Finnmark."

I took a gulp from the cup. It really did taste terrible, even if the first drink had numbed my tastebuds.

"I've been thinking, Ulf. About what a man like you is doing in a little cabin in Kåsund. You're not hunting. You haven't come for peace and quiet, or you would have said so. So what is it?"

"What do you think the weather's going to do?" I refilled his cup. "More wind? Less sun?"

"Forgive me asking, but you're on the run from someone. The police? Or do you owe someone money?"

I yawned. "How did you know the drink wasn't for Knut's father?"

A frown appeared on his broad, low forehead. "Hugo?"

"I could smell his workroom. He's not a teetotaler."

"You've been in his room? Did Lea let you inside the house?"

Lea. Her name was Lea.

"You, an unbeliever? Now that—" He suddenly broke off, his face cracked into a smile, and he leaned forward with a laugh as he slapped me on my bad shoulder. "That's it! Women! You're one of those, a horny fucker. You've got a married man after you, haven't you?"

I rubbed my shoulder. "How did you know?"

Mattis pointed at his narrow, slanted eyes. "We Sámi are children of the earth, you know. You Norwegians follow the path of reason, whereas we're just foolish shamans who don't understand, but we *sense* things, we *see.*"

"Lea just lent me this rifle," I said. "Until her husband comes back from fishing."

Mattis looked at me. His jaw was going up and down in a grinding semicircle. He took a tiny sip from the cup. "In that case you can keep hold of it for a good while."

"Oh?"

"You were wondering how I knew the drink wasn't

for Hugo. That's because he's not coming home from fishing." Another little sip. "Word came through this morning that they'd found his life jacket." He looked up at me. "Lea didn't mention it? No, I don't suppose she would have. The parish has been praying for Hugo for the past fortnight. They—the Læstadians—think that means he'll be saved, no matter how bad the weather has been out at sea. Anything else would be sacrilegious."

I nodded. So that's what Knut had meant when he told me his mother was lying when she said he didn't have to worry about his father.

"But now they're let off," Mattis said. "Now they can say that God has sent them a sign."

"So the coast guards found his life jacket this morning?"

"The coast guards?" Mattis laughed. "No, they stopped looking more than a week ago. Another fisherman found the life jacket in the water west of Hvassøya." He looked and saw the questioning expression on my face. "The fishermen write their names on the inside of their life jackets. Life jackets float better than fishermen. That way the next of kin get to know for certain."

"Tragic," I said.

He stared out into space with a distracted look. "Oh, there are plenty worse tragedies than being Hugo Eliassen's widow."

"What do you mean by that?"

"Who knows?" He looked pointedly at his empty cup. I don't know why he was so eager to drink, he must have had crates of the stuff at home. Maybe the raw materials were expensive. I filled his cup. He moistened his lips with the drink.

"Pardon me," he said, and let out a fart. "Well, the Eliassen brothers were real hotheads even when they were young. They learned to fight early. They learned to drink early. And they learned how to get what they wanted early. And they learned all this from their father, of course; he had two boats and eight men working on them. And Lea was the prettiest young girl in Kåsund back then, with her long black hair and those eyes. Even with that scar. Her father, Jakob the pastor, watched her like a hawk. You know, if a Læstadian fucks outside of marriage, it's straight to hell with the lot of them, boy, girl and offspring. Not that Lea didn't know how to look after herself. She's strong, and she knows what she wants. But obviously, against Hugo Eliassen . . ." He sighed deeply. Turned the cup in his hands.

I waited until I realised he was expecting me to prompt him. "What happened?"

"No one but the two of them really knows. But all the same, it was a bit odd. She was eighteen years old and had never given him a second glance, he was twenty-four and furious, because he thought she ought to worship the ground he walked on, seeing as he was heir to a couple of fishing boats. There was a drunken party at the Eliassens' and a prayer meeting in the Læstadians' hall. Lea walked home alone. It was during the dark season, so no one saw anything, but someone said they heard Lea and Hugo's voices, then there was a scream, followed by silence. And a month later Hugo was standing at the altar dressed up to the nines, watching Jakob Sara, who was walking his daughter down the aisle with an icy expression. She had tears in her eyes and bruises on her neck and cheek. And I have to say, that was the last time anyone saw bruises on her." He drained his cup and got to his feet. "But what do I know, I'm just a wretched Sámi, maybe they were happy the whole way through. Someone must end up happy, because people are always getting married. And that's why I need to be getting home, because I've got to deliver the drink for the wedding in Kåsund in three days' time. Are you going?"

"Me? I'm afraid I haven't been invited."

"No one needs an invitation, everyone's welcome here. Have you been to a Sámi wedding before?"

I shook my head.

"Then you ought to come. A party lasting three days, if not longer. Good food, randy women and Mattis's drink."

"Thanks, but I've got a lot I need to get done here."

"Here?" He chuckled and put his hat on. "You'll end up coming, Ulf. Three days alone on the plateau is lonelier than you think. The stillness does something to you, especially to someone who's been living in Oslo for a few years."

It struck me that he knew what he was talking about. Leaving aside the fact that I couldn't remember ever telling him where I was from.

When we went outside the buck was standing just ten metres away from the cabin. It raised its head and looked at me. Then it was as if it realised how close I was, backed up a couple of steps, then turned and lumbered off.

"Didn't you say the reindeer up here were tame?" I said.

"No reindeer's completely tame," Mattis said. "But even that one has an owner. The mark on its ear tells you who stole it."

"What's that clicking sound it makes when it runs?"

"That's the tendons in its knees. Good alarm if the married man shows up, eh?" He laughed out loud.

I have to admit that the same thought had occurred to me: the buck was a good watchdog.

"See you at the wedding, Ulf. The ceremony's at ten o'clock, and I can guarantee that it'll be beautiful."

"Thanks, but I don't think so."

"Okay, then. Goodbye, good day and farewell.

And if you're going anywhere, I wish you a safe trip." He spat. The lump was so heavy that the heather sank beneath it. He carried on chuckling to himself as he rolled away in the direction of the village. "And if you get ill"—he called over his shoulder—"I wish you a speedy recovery."

CHAPTER 6

Tick-tock, tick-tock.

I stared at the horizon. Mostly in the direction of Kåsund. But they might take the long way round, through the woods, and attack me from the rear.

I only let myself have little shots, but even so I finished the first bottle during the course of the first day. I managed to wait partway into the next day before opening the second one.

My eyes were stinging worse now. When I eventually lay down on the bed and closed my eyes, I told myself that I would hear the reindeer's knee tendons if anyone approached.

Instead I heard church bells.

At first I couldn't work out what it was. It was carried on the wind, a thin remnant of a sound. But then—when the gentle breeze was blowing steadily from the village—I heard it more clearly. Bells ringing. I looked at the time. Eleven. Did that mean it was Sunday? I decided it was, and that I would keep track of what day it was from now on. Because they would come on a weekday. On a working day.

I kept drifting off to sleep. I couldn't help it. It was like being alone on a boat on the open sea—you fall asleep and just hope you don't hit anything or capsize. Maybe that's why I dreamed I was rowing a boat full of fish. Fish that would save Anna. I was in a hurry, but the wind was blowing off the land, and I rowed and rowed, pulled at the oars until I wore the skin off my hands and the blood meant I couldn't grip them properly, so I ripped my shirt up and wound strips of fabric round the oars. I fought against the wind and current, but I was getting no closer to land. So what good was it that the boat was full to the gunwales with lovely fat fish?

The third night. I woke up wondering if the howling I had heard was a dream or reality. Either way, the dog, or whatever it was, was closer. I went out for a pee and looked at the sun as it shuffled over the clump of trees. More of the disc was behind the thin treetops than yesterday.

I had a drink and managed to fall asleep for another couple of hours.

I got up, made coffee, buttered a slice of bread and went and sat outside. I don't know if it was the oil or the alcohol in my blood, but the midges had finally got fed up with me. I tried to entice the buck to come closer with a crust of bread. I looked at it through the binoculars. It raised its head and was looking back at me. Presumably it could smell me as well as I could see it. I waved. Its ears twitched, but apart from that its expression remained unchanged. Like the landscape. Its jaws kept churning like a cement mixer. A ruminant. Like Mattis.

I searched along the horizon with the binoculars. I smeared damp ash on the lens of the rifle. I looked at the time. Maybe they would wait until it was darker so that they could creep up on me unseen. I had to sleep. I had to get hold of some Valium.

He came to the door at half past six one morning.

The doorbell almost didn't wake me up. Valium and earplugs. And pyjamas. All year round. The useless old single-glazed windows in the flat let everything in: autumn storms, winter cold, birdsong and the sound of that bastard garbage truck which backed up into the entrance to the courtyard three days a week—right under my bedroom window on the first floor, in other words.

God knows, I had enough in that damn money belt to get proper double glazing, or move one floor higher up, but all the money in the world couldn't bring back what I'd lost. And since the funeral I hadn't managed to do anything. Apart from changing the lock. I'd installed a fuck-off great German lock. There had never been a break-in here before, but God knows why not.

He looked like a boy dressed up in one of his dad's suits. A scrawny neck stuck up above his shirt, topped by a big head with a wispy fringe.

"Yes?"

"The Fisherman's sent me."

"Okay." I felt myself go cold, despite the pyjamas. "And who are you?"

"I'm new, my name's Johnny Moe."

"Okay, Johnny. You could have waited until nine o'clock, then you'd have found me in the back room at the shop. Dressed and everything."

"I'm here about Gustavo King . . ."

Fuck.

"Can I come in?"

As I considered his request I looked at the bulge in

the left-hand side of his tweed jacket. A large pistol. Maybe that was why he was wearing such a big jacket.

"Just to clear things up," he said. "The Fisherman insists."

Refusing to let him in would have looked suspicious. And pointless.

"Of course," I said, opening the door. "Coffee?"

"I only drink tea."

"I'm afraid I haven't got any tea."

He pushed his fringe to one side. The nail on his forefinger was long. "I didn't say I wanted any, Mr. Hansen, just that that is what I drink. Is this the living room? Please, after you."

I went in, shoved some copies of *Mad* and a few Mingus and Monica Zetterlund albums off one of the chairs and sat down. He sank down on the wrecked springs of the sofa next to the guitar. Sank so low that he had to move the empty vodka bottle on the table to see me properly. And get a clear line of fire.

"Mr. Gustavo King's body was found yesterday," he said. "But not in Bunnefjorden, where you told the Fisherman you'd dumped it. The only thing that matched was that he had a bullet in his head."

"Shit, has the body been moved? Where . . . ?"

"Salvador, in Brazil."

I nodded slowly.

"Who . . . ?"

"Me," he said, sticking his right hand inside his jacket. "With this." It wasn't a pistol, it was a revolver. Big, black, and nasty. And the Valium had worn off. "The day before yesterday. He was definitely alive up to then."

I carried on nodding slowly. "How did you find him?"

"When you sit in a bar in Salvador every night boasting about how you managed to make a fool out of the drug king of Norway, the drug king of Norway is going to find out about it sooner or later."

"Silly of him."

"But having said that, we'd have found him anyway."

"Even if you believed he was dead?"

"The Fisherman never stops looking for his debtors until he sees the corpse. Never." Johnny's thin lips curled into a hint of a smile. "And the Fisherman always finds what he's looking for. You and I may not know how, but he knows. Always. That's why he's called the Fisherman."

"Did Gustavo say anything before you—?"

"Mr. King confessed everything. That's why I shot him in the head."

"What?"

Johnny Moe made a gesture as if to shrug his shoulders, but it was barely visible in his outsized suit. "I gave him the option of quick or drawn out. If he didn't lay his cards on the table, it would be drawn out. I'm assuming that you, as a fixer, are aware of the effects of a well-placed shot to the gut. Stomach acid in the spleen and liver . . ."

I nodded. Even if I had no idea what he was talking about, I did have a certain amount of imagination.

"The Fisherman wanted me to give you the same choice."

"If I c-c-confess?" My teeth were chattering.

"If you give us back the money and drugs that Mr. King stole from the Fisherman, which you received half of."

I nodded. The disadvantage of the Valium wearing off was that I was terrified, and it's seriously fucking painful being terrified. The advantage was that I was actually capable of a degree of thought. And it occurred to me that this was a direct copy of the attack-at-dawn scenario with me and Gustavo. So how about me copying Gustavo?

"We can split it," I said.

"Like you and Gustavo did?" Johnny said. "So you end up like him, and me like you? No, thanks." He brushed his fringe aside. His fingernail scratched the skin on his forehead. Put me in mind of an eagle's claw. "Quick or drawn out, Mr. Hansen?"

I swallowed. Think, think. But instead of a solution, all I saw was my life—my choices, my bad choices—passing by. As I sat there quietly I heard a diesel engine, voices, untroubled laughter outside the window. The dustbin men. Why hadn't I become a dustbin man? Honest toil, clearing up, serving society, and going home happy. Alone, but at least I could have gone to bed with a degree of satisfaction. Hang on. Bed. Maybe . . .

"I've got the money and gear in the bedroom," I said.

"Let's go."

We stood up.

"Please," he said, waving the revolver. "Age before beauty."

As we walked the few steps through the corridor to the bedroom I visualised how it would happen. I would go over to the bed with him behind me, grab the pistol. I'd turn round, not look at his face, and fire. Simple. It was him or me. I just mustn't look at his face.

We were there. I headed towards the bed. Grabbed the pillow. Grabbed the pistol. Spun round. His mouth had fallen open. Eyes wide. He knew he was going to die. I fired.

That's to say, I *meant* to fire. Every fibre of my being wanted to fire. *Had* fired. With the exception of my right forefinger. It had happened again.

He raised his revolver and aimed it at me. "That was silly of you, Mr. Hansen."

Not *silly*, I thought. Getting the money for treatment just a week or two after the illness had progressed so far that it was too late, *that* was silly. Mixing Valium and vodka was silly. But not managing to shoot when your own life is in the balance, that's a genetic disability. I was an evolutionary aberration, and the future of humanity would only be served by my immediate extinction.

"Head shot or stomach?"

"Head," I said, and went over to the wardrobe. I got out the brown case containing the money belt and the bags of amphetamine. I turned to face him. Saw his eye above the sights of the revolver, the other one screwed shut, the eagle's claw curled round the trigger. For a moment I wondered what he was waiting for before I realised. The dustbin men. He didn't want them to hear the shot when they were standing right under the window.

Right under the window.

First floor.

Thin glass.

Perhaps my Darwinian creator hadn't deserted me after all, because as I twisted round and ran the three steps towards the window there was just one thought in my head: survival.

I can't swear that the details of what followed are entirely correct, but I think I was holding the case—or the pistol—in front of me as I penetrated and shattered the glass as if it were a soap bubble, and the next moment I was falling through the air. I hit the roof of the bin lorry with my left shoulder, rolled over, felt the sun-warmed metal against my stomach, then I slid down the side of the vehicle until my naked feet hit the ground and I was down on the tarmac.

The voices had fallen silent, and two men in brown overalls stood there frozen to the spot, just staring. I pulled up my pyjama trousers, which had slid down, and grabbed the case and pistol. I glanced up at my window. Behind a frame of broken glass, Johnny was standing looking down at me.

I nodded at him.

He gave me a crooked smile and raised the forefinger with the long nail to his forehead. A gesture which in hindsight has come to seem like a sort of salute: I had won that round. But we would meet again.

Then I turned and began to run down the street in the low morning sun.

Mattis was right.

This landscape, this tranquillity, was doing something to me.

I had spent years living on my own in Oslo, but after just three days here the isolation felt like a sort of pressure, a quiet sobbing, a thirst that neither water nor moonshine could sate. So as I stared out across the empty plateau with the grey, overcast sky above it, and no sign of the reindeer, I looked at the time.

The wedding. I had never been to a wedding before. What does that say about a thirty-five-year-old bloke? Friendless? Or simply the wrong friends, the sort of friends no one wanted, let alone wanted to marry?

So yes, I checked my reflection in the bucket of water, brushed my jacket down, tucked the pistol in my waistband at the small of my back, and set off towards Kåsund.

CHAPTER 7

I'd got far enough to be able to see the village below me when the church bells started to ring again. I speeded up. It had got colder. Maybe because it was cloudy. Maybe because the summer can come to an end up here quite suddenly.

There wasn't a soul in sight, but there were several cars parked on the gravel road in front of the church, and I could hear organ music inside. Did that mean that the bride was on her way to the altar, or was it just part of the warm-up? Like I said, I'd never seen a wedding before. I looked at the parked cars, to see if she was sitting in one of them waiting to make her entrance. I noticed that the number plates all had a Y at the front, to indicate that they were from Finnmark. All apart from one, a big, black station wagon that had no letter before the number. From Oslo.

I went up the steps to the church and cautiously opened the door. The few pews were full, but I crept in and found a place on the one at the back. The organ music paused, and I looked ahead. I couldn't see any bridal couple, so at least I was going to catch the whole thing. I could see a number of Sámi jackets in front of me, but not as many as I'd expected to see at a Sámi wedding. On the front pew I could see the backs of two heads I recognised. Knut's unruly red hair, and Lea's shimmering black cascade of locks. Hers was partially covered by a veil. From where I was sitting I couldn't see much, but presumably the bridegroom was sitting up at the front near the altar with his best man, waiting for the bride. There was a bit of murmuring and coughing and crying. There was something rather appealing about such a reserved, sombre congregation that was still so easily moved on behalf of the bridal couple.

Knut turned round and looked at the gathering. I tried to catch his eye, but he didn't see me, or at least didn't return my smile.

The organ started up again, and the congregation joined in with astonishing gusto. *"Nearer, my God, to Thee . . ."*

Not that I knew much about hymns, but that one struck me as an odd choice for a wedding. And I had never heard it sung so slowly. The congregation stretched out all the vowels to their breaking point: *"Nearer to Thee, e'en though it be a cross that raiseth me."*

After something like five verses I closed my eyes. Possibly out of sheer boredom, but possibly because of the feeling of security from being among a crowd after so many days of watchfulness. Either way: I fell asleep.

And woke up to the strains of a southern accent.

I wiped the drool from the corners of my mouth. Perhaps someone had nudged me on my bad shoulder—it was aching, anyway. I rubbed my eyes. Saw little yellow crusts of sleep on my fingertips. I squinted. The man speaking in a southern accent up at the front had glasses and thin, colourless hair, and he was wearing the cassock I had slept under.

"... but he was also someone who had weaknesses," he said. *Weaknesses.* "The sort we all have. He was a man who was capable of fleeing from confrontation when he had sinned, who lost his bearings and hoped problems would simply vanish if he stayed out of the way long enough. But we all know that we can't hide from the punishment of the Lord, that He will always find us. But he is also one of Jesus's lost sheep, one who has strayed from the flock, one whom Jesus Christ wants to rescue and save with his mercy if the sinner prays for the forgiveness of the Lord when death comes."

This wasn't a wedding sermon. Nor was there any bridal couple at the altar. I sat up in the pew and craned my neck. And then I saw it, right in front of the altar. A large coffin.

"Even so, perhaps he was hoping to forget his past when he set out on his last journey. That his debts would expire, that a line would be drawn under his sins without him having to pay. But he was gathered in, the way we shall all be."

I glanced at the exit. Two men were standing on either side of the door with their hands folded in front of them. They were both staring at me. Black suits. Fixers' outfits. The station wagon from Oslo outside. I had been tricked. Mattis had been sent up to the cabin to lure me from my stronghold and down into the village. To a funeral.

"And that is why we stand here today with this empty coffin . . ."

My funeral. An empty coffin waiting for me.

Sweat broke out on my forehead. What was their plan, how was it going to happen? Were they going to wait until the ceremony was over, or was I going to be despatched in here, in front of everyone?

I slipped one hand behind me and made sure that the pistol was there. Should I try to shoot my way out? Or cause a scene, stand up and point at the pair by the door, shouting that they were killers from Oslo, sent by a drug dealer? But what good would that do if the villagers had come here voluntarily to attend the funeral of a stranger from the south? The Fisherman must have paid the villagers; he had even managed to get Lea to go along with the conspiracy. Or, if what she said was true, and they didn't pay too much heed to earthly possessions here in the village, maybe the Fisherman's people had started a rumour about me, saying I was the devil incarnate. God knows how they'd managed it, but I knew I had to get away.

Out of the corner of my eye I saw one of the two fixers turn to the other and mutter something. This was my chance. I grabbed the handle of the pistol and pulled the gun out from my trousers. Stood up. I had to shoot now, before they had time to turn towards me, so I wouldn't have to see their faces.

" . . . for Hugo Eliassen, who set out to sea alone even though the weather was bad. To fish for pollock, he said. Or to flee from his unresolved deeds."

I sat down heavily on the pew again, and tucked the pistol back inside my waistband.

"We must hope that as a Christian he fell to his

knees on his boat and prayed, pleaded for forgiveness, begged to be let into the Kingdom of Heaven. Many of you here knew Hugo better than I did, but the people I have spoken to say that they believe he would have done just that, because he was a God-fearing man, and I trust that Jesus, our shepherd, heard him and brought him back into the flock."

Only now did I realise how hard my heart was pounding, as if it was going to burst out of my chest.

The congregation began to sing again.

"The pure and mighty flock."

Someone handed me an open copy of Landstad's hymnbook and pointed at the yellowed page with a friendly nod. I joined in with the second verse. Out of sheer relief and gratitude, I thanked providence for letting me live at least a little longer.

I stood outside the church watching the black station wagon drive off with the coffin.

"Well," said an elderly man who had stopped beside me. "A watery grave is better than no grave."

"Hmm."

"You'll be the one staying in the hunting cabin," he said, and looked across at me. "So, are you getting any grouse?"

"Not many."

"No, we'd have heard the gun going off," he said. "Sound carries a long way in weather like this."

I nodded. "Why did the hearse have Oslo number plates?"

"Oh, that's just Aronsen, he's a proper show-off. He bought it down there, I daresay he thinks that makes it look smarter."

Lea was standing on the church steps with a tall, fair-haired man. The queue of people wishing to convey their condolences had been quickly dealt with. Just before the car was out of sight she called: "Well, you're all welcome to come to ours for coffee. Thank you all for coming, and safe journey home to those not joining us."

It struck me that there was something strangely familiar about the image of her standing next to that man, as if I had seen it before. There was a gust of wind and the tall man swayed slightly.

"Who's that standing next to the widow?" I asked.

"Ove? He's the deceased's brother."

Of course. The wedding photograph. That must have been taken in exactly the same place, on the steps of the church.

"Twin brother?"

"Twins in every way," the old man said. "So, shall we go and have coffee and cake, then?"

"Have you seen Mattis?"

"Which Mattis?"

So there was more than one.

"Do you mean Drink-Mattis?"

Only one of them, then.

"He's probably at Migal's wedding down in Ceavccageadge today."

"Sorry?"

"Transteinsletta—down by the cod-liver-oil stone." He pointed towards the sea, where I remembered seeing the jetty. "The heathens worship their false idols down there." He shuddered. "Shall we go, then?"

In the silence that followed I thought I could hear the distant sound of drums, music. Hubbub. Drinking. Women.

I turned round and saw Lea from behind as she was heading up towards the house. She was clasping Knut's hand in hers. The dead man's brother and the others followed at a distance, in a silent procession. I ran my tongue round my mouth, which still felt dry from my nap. From having been so frightened. From all the drinking, perhaps.

"Some coffee would be good," I said.

The house seemed so different when it was full of people.

I nodded my way past people I didn't know, who

followed me with their eyes and unspoken questions.
Everyone else seemed to know each other. I found her
in the kitchen, where she was slicing cake.

"Condolences," I said.

She looked at my outstretched hand and switched
the knife to her left hand. Sun-warmed stones.
Firm gaze. "Thanks. How are you getting on in the
cabin?"

"Fine, thanks, I'm on my way there now. I just
wanted to pass on my sympathies seeing as I didn't
manage to at the church."

"You don't have to leave straight away, Ulf. Have
a bit of cake."

I looked at the cake. I didn't like cake. Never had.
My mother used to say I was an unusual child.

"Yes, well," I said, "thanks very much."

People had started to pour in behind us, so I took
the plate and cake into the living room. I ended up
over by the window, where, overwhelmed by the
intense, silent scrutiny, I peered up at the sky, as if I
were worried it was going to start raining.

"The peace of God."

I turned round. Apart from a splash of grey at the
temples, the man in front of me had her black hair.
And her direct, courageous gaze. I didn't know what
to reply. Simply repeating "The peace of God" would
have been fake, but "Hello" felt far too informal,

almost a bit cheeky. So I ended up with a stiff "Good day," even if it was an unsuitable greeting for such an occasion.

"I'm Jakob Sara."

"Iulf . . . Er, Ulf Hansen."

"My grandson says you tell jokes."

"He does?"

"But he wasn't able to tell me what your profession is. Or what you're doing here in Kåsund. Just that you've got my son-in-law's rifle. And that you're not a man of faith."

I nodded blandly, the sort of nod that is neither confirmation nor denial, but which merely acknowledges that you've heard what is being said, then stuffed a large piece of cake into my mouth to give myself a few seconds to think. I went on chewing and nodding.

"And that's none of my business either," the man continued. "Not that, and not how long you're thinking of staying here. But I can see for myself that you like almond cake."

He looked me hard in the eye as I struggled to swallow. Then he put a hand on my bad shoulder. "Remember, young man, that God's mercy is boundless." He paused, and I felt the warmth of his hand spread through the fabric and into my skin. "Almost."

He smiled and walked away, moving on to

another of the mourners, and I heard their muttered exchange of "The peace of God."

"Ulf?"

I didn't have to turn round to know who it was.

"Shall we play secret hiding?" He was looking up at me with a serious face.

"Knut, I'm—"

"Please!"

"Hmm." I looked down at the remnants of the cake. "What's secret hiding?"

"Hiding so that no grown-ups know you're hiding. You're not allowed to run or shout or laugh, and you're not allowed to hide in silly places. We play it when we're at parish meetings. It's good fun. I'll look first."

I looked around. There were no other children here, just Knut. Alone at his father's funeral. Secret hiding. Why not?

"I'll count to thirty-three," he whispered. "From now."

He turned to face the wall, as if he were looking at his parents' wedding picture, while I put my plate down and discreetly made my way out of the living room and through the corridor. I glanced in the kitchen, but she was no longer there. I went outside. The wind was getting up. I walked round the old car. A few raindrops hit the windscreen as the wind gusted past. I carried on round the back of the house. I leaned against the wall beneath the open window of the workroom. Lit a cigarette.

It was only when the wind died down that I heard the voices in the workroom:

"Let go, Ove! You've been drinking, you don't know what you're saying."

"Don't struggle, Lea. You shouldn't mourn too long, Hugo wouldn't want that."

"You don't know what Hugo would want!"

"Well, I know what *I* want. And always have wanted. And so do you."

"Let go now, Ove. Or I'll shout."

"The way you shouted that night with Hugo?" Hoarse, drunken laughter. "You argue a lot, Lea, but in the end you back down and obey your menfolk. Like you obeyed Hugo, and like you obeyed your father. And like you're going to obey me."

"Never!"

"That's the way we do it in our family, Lea. Hugo was my brother, now he's gone, and you and Knut are my responsibility."

"Ove, that's enough now."

"Just ask your father."

In the silence that followed, I wondered if I should move.

I stayed where I was.

"You're a widow and a mother, Lea. Be sensible. Hugo and I shared everything—this is what he would have wanted, I promise you. And it's what *I* want. Now, come here, let me just . . . ow! Fucking women!"

A door slammed.

I heard more muttered cursing. Something fell to the floor. Just then Knut came round the corner of the house. He opened his mouth wide to shout, and I steeled myself for the cry that would give me away.

But it didn't come, just the silent-movie version.

Secret hiding.

I tossed the cigarette away, hurried towards him and threw out my arms in resignation. I led him towards the garage.

"I'll count to thirty-three," I said, then turned to face his mother's red Volkswagen. I heard his footsteps run off, then the front door open.

When I finished counting, I went back inside.

She was standing on her own in the kitchen again, peeling potatoes.

"Hi," I said quietly.

She looked up. Her cheeks were red, her eyes shiny.

"Sorry," she said with a sniff.

"You could have got some help to make dinner today."

"Oh, they all offered. But it's better to keep yourself busy, I think."

"Yes, maybe you're right," I said, sitting down at the kitchen table. I noticed her stiffen slightly. "You don't have to say anything," I said. "I just wanted to sit down for a while before I left, and in there . . . well, I haven't got much to talk to anyone about."

"Apart from Knut."

"Oh, he does most of the talking. Clever boy. He's done a lot of thinking for someone his age."

"He's had plenty to think about." She wiped her nose with the back of her hand.

"Yes."

I felt I was about to say something, that the words were on their way, I just wasn't quite sure which ones they were going to be. And when they arrived it was as if they had arranged themselves, that I wasn't in charge of them, yet they were still born of the clearest logic.

"If you'd like to be on your own with Knut," I said, "but aren't sure if you could manage, I'd really like to help you."

I looked down at my hands. Heard the peeling stop.

"I don't know how long I've got to live," I said. "And I haven't got any family. No heirs."

"What are you saying, Ulf?"

Yes, what exactly was I saying? Had these thoughts appeared in the few minutes that had passed since I had been standing beneath the window?

"Just that if I disappear, then you should look behind the loose plank to the left of the wall cupboard up there," I said. "Behind the moss."

She let the potato peeler fall into the sink and was looking at me with a concerned expression on her face. "Are you ill, Ulf?"

I shook my head.

She stared at me with that distant, blue look in her eyes. The look Ove had seen, and had drowned in. He must have done.

"Then I'm not sure you should think like that," she said. "And Knut and I will be fine, so don't worry about that either. If you're looking for something to spend your money on, there are plenty of people in the village who are worse off."

I felt my cheeks flush. She turned her back on me and started peeling again. She stopped again when she heard my chair scrape.

"But thanks for coming," she said. "Seeing you cheered Knut up."

"No, thank you," I said, and headed towards the door.

"And . . ."

"Yes?"

"There's a prayer meeting here in two days' time. Six o'clock. Like I said, you'd be very welcome."

I found Knut in what I assumed was his room. His

thin legs stuck out from under his bed. He was wearing a pair of soccer boots that had to be at least two sizes too small. He giggled as I pulled him out and dropped him down on top of the bed.

"I'm off now," I said.

"Already? But . . ."

"Have you got a ball?"

He nodded, but his bottom lip was pouting.

"Good, then you can practise your kicking against the garage wall. Draw a circle, aim as hard as you can, then stop the ball as it comes back. If you do that a thousand times, you'll be much better than the others in the team when they come home after the summer."

"I'm not on the team."

"You will be, if you do that."

"I'm not on the team because I'm not allowed to be."

"Not allowed?"

"Mum says I can, but Grandpa says sport takes your attention away from God, that the rest of the world can spend Sundays shouting and yelling and running after a ball, but for us Sunday belongs to the Word."

"I see," I lied. "And what did your father say about that?"

The lad shrugged. "Nothing."

"Nothing?"

"He didn't care. All he cared about ..." Knut stopped. He had tears in his eyes. I put my arm round his shoulders. I didn't need to hear it. Because I already knew, I'd met plenty of Hugos, some of them had been my customers. And I myself was fond of that sort of escape, I needed that outlet. It was just that as I sat there feeling the boy lean against me, the mute sobbing that rocked his warm body, I couldn't help thinking that *that* had to be something no father could run away from, would even *want* to escape. That it was a blessing and a curse that strapped you firmly to the tiller. But who was I to say anything about that, I who—whether or not of my own accord—had abandoned ship before she had even been born? I let go of Knut.

"You're coming to the prayer meeting?" he said.

"I don't know. But I've got another job for you."

"Okay!"

"It's like secret hiding, it's all about not saying anything, not to anyone."

"Great!"

"How often does the bus come?"

"Four times a day. Two from the south, two from the east. Two during the day, two at night."

"Okay. I want you to be there when the daytime bus from the south arrives. If anyone you don't know gets off, you come straight to me. You don't run, you don't shout, you don't say anything. Same thing if a car with Oslo plates arrives. Do you get it? I'll give you five kroner each time."

"Like a . . . spy mission?"

"Something like that, yes."

"Are they the people who are going to bring your shotgun?"

"See you, Knut." I tousled his hair and stood up.

On the way out I met the tall, fair-haired man as he stumbled out of the toilet. I heard the water flush behind him as he was still fumbling with his belt. He raised his head and looked at me. Ove Eliassen.

"The peace of God," I said.

I could feel his heavy, drink-soused gaze on my back.

I came to a stop a short way down the road. The sound of drums was carrying on the wind. But I had already sated my hunger, I'd fulfilled my need to see other people.

"I think it's time for me to go home and have a good cry," Toralf would sometimes say late in the evening. That always made the other drinkers chuckle. That it happened to be precisely what Toralf did was another matter.

"Put on that angry bloke of yours," he would say when we got home. "Let's take a trip into the depths." I don't know if he actually liked Charles Mingus, or any of my other jazz records, for that matter, or if he just wanted the company of another miserable bastard. But occasionally Toralf and I would enter the black of night at the same time.

"Now we're properly miserable!" he would laugh.

Toralf and I called it the black hole. I'd read about a guy called Finkelstein who had discovered that there were holes in space which would suck everything in if you got too close, even light, and that they were so black they were impossible to observe with the naked eye. And that was exactly what it was like. You couldn't see anything, you were just getting on with your life, and then one day you could just physically feel that you'd got caught in the gravitational field, and then you were lost, you got sucked into a black hole of hopelessness and infinite despair. And in there everything was the mirror image of the way it was outside. You'd keep asking yourself if there was any reason to have any hope, if there was any good reason *not* to despair. It was a hole in which you just had to let time run its course, put on a record by another depressed soul, the angry man of jazz, Charles Mingus, and hope you emerged on the other side, like some fucking Alice popping out of her rabbit hole. But according to Finkelstein and the others, that might be exactly what it was like, that there was a sort of mirror-image wonderland on the other side of the black hole. I don't know, but it strikes me that it's as good and reliable a religion as any other.

I looked over to where I knew the path ran. At the landscape that seemed to rise up and vanish into the clouds. Somewhere in there, the long night started.

CHAPTER 8

Bobby was one of the girls in Slottsparken. She had very long brown hair and dark eyes, and she smoked hash. That's obviously an extremely superficial description of anyone, but those are the first things I think of. She didn't say much, but she smoked a lot, which made her eyes soft. We were fairly similar. Her real name was Borgny, and she was from a wealthy family in the western suburbs. Well, she wasn't quite as wealthy as she liked to make out; she just liked the idea of the rebellious hippy chick breaking away from social conservatism, financial security and right-wing politics for ... well, what? To test some naive ideas about how to live life, expand her consciousness and break from old-fashioned convention. Such as the convention that when a man and a woman have a child together, that brings with it a certain responsibility for both parties. Like I said, we were fairly similar.

We were sitting in Slottsparken, listening to a guy play a dodgy version of "The Times They Are A-Changin'" on an untuned guitar when Bobby told me she was pregnant. And that she was pretty sure I was the father.

"Cool, we're going to be parents," I said, trying not to look as though someone had just tipped a bucket of ice-cold water over my head.

"You just have to pay maintenance," she said.

"Well, obviously I'll be happy to do my bit. We'll do this together."

"Together is right," she said. "But not together with you."

"Oh? So . . . together with who, then?"

"Me and Ingvald," she said, nodding towards the guy with the guitar. "We're together now, and he says he'd like to be a father. As long as you pay maintenance, of course."

And that's what happened. Okay, so Ingvald didn't hang around for long. By the time Anna was born Bobby was with another bloke whose name started with *I*. I think it might have been Ivar. I was allowed to see Anna very occasionally, at irregular intervals, but there was never any discussion of me looking after her. Nor did I think that was what I wanted either, not then. Not because I didn't care—I fell in love with her the moment I first set eyes on her. Her eyes radiated a sort of blue shimmer as she lay in her pram gurgling and looking up at me, and even if I didn't really know her, she became the most valuable thing in my life overnight.

Maybe that was why. She was so small and fragile, but so precious that I didn't want to look after her on my own. I couldn't. I didn't dare. Because I was bound to do something wrong, something irrevocable. I was sure I would do lasting damage to Anna one way or another. Not that I'm an irresponsible or careless person, I've just got really bad judgement. That's why I was always prepared to follow the advice given by random strangers, and leave important decisions to other people. Even when I knew that they—in this case Bobby—were no better than me. *Cowardly* is probably the word I'm looking for. So I kept out of the way, sold hash, and gave Bobby half the money once a week, when I would look down into the magical blue shimmer of Anna's smiling eyes, and maybe even get to hold her when we were having coffee if Bobby was between men.

I told Bobby that if she could stay away from Slottsparken and dope, I'd keep away from the cops, from the Fisherman, from trouble. Because she and Anna wouldn't be able to manage if I ended up behind bars. Like I said, Bobby's parents weren't actually that rich, but were so middle class and conservative that they'd made it very clear that they wanted nothing to do with their hash-smoking, promiscuous hippy daughter, and that she and the child's father would have to fend for themselves, possibly with the help of the state.

Finally the day came when Bobby said she couldn't handle looking after the bloody kid any more. Anna had been crying, her nose bleeding, and she had been running a fever for four days in a row. When I looked down at the bed, the blue light in her eyes had been replaced by blue circles beneath them; she was pale and had strange blue bruises on her knees and elbows. I took her to the doctor's, and three days later came the diagnosis. Acute leukaemia. A one-way ticket to death. The doctors gave her four months. Everyone kept saying that things like that just happened, lightning striking at random, mercilessly, pointlessly.

I flew into a rage, asked questions, made phone calls, checked, went to see specialists, and eventually found out that there was a treatment for leukaemia in Germany. It didn't save everyone, and it cost a fortune, but it gave one thing: hope. Sensibly, the Norwegian state had other things to spend its money on than fragile hope, and Bobby's parents said it was fate, and a matter for the Norwegian health service; they weren't paying for some fantasy cure from Naziland. I did the sums. If I sold five times as much hash, I still wouldn't make enough in time. Even so, I tried, I worked eighteen-hour shifts and pushed like mad for sales, heading down towards the cathedral when the Slottsparken fell silent at night. When I next went to the hospital they asked why no one had been there for the past three days.

"Hasn't Bobby been here?"

The nurse and doctor shook their heads, said they'd tried calling her, but that her phone seemed to have been cut off.

When I got to Bobby's she was lying in bed and said she was ill, and that it was my fault she couldn't afford to pay the phone bill. I went to the toilet and was about to drop a cigarette butt in the bin when I saw the bloody cotton-wool ball. Further down in the bin I found a syringe. Maybe I'd been half-expecting it to happen; I'd seen more fragile souls than Bobby cross that line.

So what did I do?

I did nothing.

I left Bobby there, tried to convince myself that Anna was better off with the nurses than with either of her parents, and I sold hash and saved up for that bastard miracle cure I forced myself to believe in because the alternative was unbearable, because my fear that the little girl with the blue light in her eyes would die was even stronger than my own fear of death. Because we take comfort where we can find it: in a German medical journal, in a syringe full of heroin, in a shiny new book promising eternal life as long as you subordinate yourself to whatever new saviour they've just come up with. So I sold hash and counted the kroner, and counted the days.

That was the situation when the Fisherman offered me a job.

Two days. The clouds were hanging low, but weren't letting go of any rain. The earth turned, but I didn't see the sun. The hours were, if possible, even more monotonous. I tried to sleep through them, but that turned out to be impossible without Valium.

I was going mad. More mad. Knut had been right. *There's nothing worse than not knowing when the bullet's coming.*

Towards the evening of the second day I'd had enough.

Mattis had said the wedding would carry on for three days.

I washed in the stream. I no longer noticed the midges. They only annoyed me now when they landed on my eyes, in my mouth or on a piece of bread. And my shoulder no longer hurt. It was funny, but when I woke up the day after the funeral the pain was gone. I'd cast my mind back, tried to remember if I'd done anything in particular, but I couldn't think of anything.

After washing I rinsed my shirt, wrung it out and put it on. I hoped it would be passably dry by the time I reached the village. I wondered whether or not I should take the pistol. In the end I decided to leave it, and hid it behind the moss alongside the money belt. I looked at the rifle and box of ammunition. I thought about what Mattis had said. That the only reason no one ever stole anything in Kåsund was that there was nothing worth stealing. There wasn't room for the rifle behind the plank, so I wrapped it in some roofing felt I found under the bunk and hid it beneath four big stones over by the stream.

Then I left.

Even if the wind was gusty, there was something heavy in the air that seemed to press at my temples. As if there was thunder on the way. Maybe the celebrations were already over. The drink finished. The available women taken. But as I got closer I heard the same drums I'd heard two days before. I walked past the church towards the jetty. Followed the sound.

I turned off the road and headed east, up onto a hill. Before me a stony grey desert of a headland stretched

out towards a steel-blue sea. At the neck of the headland, immediately below me, lay a flat, well-trodden
patch of ground, and that was where they were dancing. A large fire was burning alongside a five- or six-
metre-high obelisk-like rock that stuck up from the
ground. Around it lay two circles of smaller stones.
There wasn't any real symmetry to the stones, no rec-
ognisable pattern, but they still looked like the foun-
dations of a building that had never been finished. Or
rather a building site that had decayed, been demol-
ished or torched. I walked down towards them.

"Hello!" yelled a tall, fair-haired youth in a Sámi
jacket who was having a piss on the heather at the edge
of the clearing. "Who are you?"

"Ulf."

"The southerner! Better late than never—welcome!"
He shook his cock, scattering drops in all directions,
stuffed it back in his trousers and held out his hand.
"Kornelius, Mattis's second cousin! Oh, yes."

I was reluctant to take his hand.

"So that's the cod-liver-oil stone," I said. "Is it a
ruined temple?"

"Transteinen?" Kornelius shook his head. "No,
Beaive-Vuolab threw it there."

"Really? And who's that then?"

"A pretty strong Sámi. A demigod, maybe. No,
quarter! A quarter-god."

"Hmm. And why do quarter-gods chuck rocks here?"

"Why does anyone chuck heavy rocks? To prove that they can, of course!" He laughed. "Why didn't you come earlier, Ulf? The party's almost over now."

"I got it wrong, I thought the wedding was in the church."

"What, with that superstitious lot?" He pulled out a hip flask. "Mattis is better at marrying people than those thin-blooded Lutherans."

"Really? So which gods is it done in the name of, then?" I peered towards the fires and a long table. A girl in a green dress had stopped dancing and was looking at me curiously. Even from a distance I could tell she had a fine figure.

"Gods? No gods, he marries them in the name of the Norwegian state."

"Is he authorised to do that?"

"Oh, yes. He's one of three people in the district who are." Kornelius raised a clenched fist and unfolded his fingers one by one: "The priest, the deputy judge, and the ship's captain."

"Wow. So Mattis is a ship's captain as well?"

"Mattis?" Kornelius laughed and took a swig from the hip flask. "Does he look like a seagoing Sámi? Have you seen him walk? No, Eliassen senior's the captain, and he can only marry people on board his boats, and no women have ever set foot on one. Oh, yes."

"So what do you mean, have I seen Mattis walk?"

"Only nomadic Sámi are that bow-legged, not sea-going Sámi."

"Really?"

"Fish." He passed me the hip flask. "They don't eat fish inland on the plateau. So they don't get enough iodine. They get soft bones." He stuck his knees out by way of illustration.

"And you're . . ."

"Fake Sámi. My father was from Bergen, but don't tell anyone. Especially not my mother."

He laughed, and I couldn't help joining in. The drink tasted even worse than the stuff I'd got from Mattis.

"So what is he, then? A priest?"

"Almost," Kornelius said. "He went off to Oslo to study theology. But then he lost his faith. So he switched to law. He worked as a deputy judge in Tromsø for three years. Oh, yes."

"No offence, Kornelius, but unless I'm badly mistaken, something like eighty per cent of what you've told me is either lies or fantasy."

He adopted a hurt expression. "Hell, no. First Mattis lost his faith in God. Then he lost his faith in the legal system. And now the only thing he believes in is alcohol content, or so he says." Kornelius laughed loudly and slapped my back so hard that the drink almost came back up again. Which might actually have been a good thing.

"What sort of hellish brew is that?" I asked, handing him the hip flask.

"*Reikas,*" he said. "Fermented reindeer milk." He shook his head sadly. "But the youth of today only want fizzy drinks and cola. Snow-scooters and hotdogs. Proper spirits, sledges and reindeer meat, all that will soon be gone. We're going to the dogs. Oh, yes." He took a consoling swig from the flask before screwing the lid on. "Ah, here comes Anita."

I watched the girl in the green dress walk towards us, apparently rather aimlessly, and straightened up automatically.

"Now, now, Ulf," Kornelius said in a low voice. "Let her do a reading for you, but nothing more."

"A reading?"

"Second sight. She's a real shaman. But you don't want what she wants."

"And that is?"

"You can see that from here."

"Hmm. Why not? Is she married? Engaged?"

"No, but you don't want what she's got."

"Got?"

"Has and spreads."

I nodded slowly.

He put his hand on my shoulder.

"But have fun. Kornelius isn't one to gossip."

He turned towards the girl. "Hi, Anita!"

"Goodbye, Kornelius."

He laughed and walked off. The girl stopped in front of me, smiling with her mouth closed. Sweaty and still out of breath from dancing. She had two angry red pimples on her forehead, pupils the size of pinpricks, and wild eyes that spoke for themselves. Dope, probably speed.

"Hi," I said.

She didn't reply, just inspected me from top to toe. I shifted my weight.

"Do you want me?" she asked.

I shook my head.

"Why not?"

I shrugged my shoulders.

"You look like a healthy specimen of a man. What's wrong?"

"I understand that you can tell things like that about people."

She laughed. "Did Kornelius say that? Oh, yes, Anita can see things. And she saw that you were keen enough a few moments ago. What happened, did you get scared?"

"It's not you, it's me, I've got a touch of syphilis."

When she laughed, I could see why she smiled without showing her teeth. "I've got rubbers."

"More than a touch, actually. My cock's fallen off."

She came a step closer. Put her hand on my crotch. "It doesn't feel like it. Come on, I live behind the church."

I shook my head and took a firm grip of her wrist.

"Fucking southerners," she hissed, and snatched her hand away from me. "What's so wrong about a quick fuck? We're all going to die soon, didn't you know?"

"Yeah, I've heard the rumours," I said, and looked round for a suitable escape route.

"You don't believe me," she said. "Look at me. *Look* at me, I said!"

I looked at her.

She smiled. "Oh, yes, Anita saw right. You've got death in your eyes. Don't turn away! Anita can see you're going to shoot the reflection. Yes, shoot the reflection."

A small alarm had gone off inside my head. "What fucking southerners are you talking about?"

"You, of course."

"Which *other* southerners?"

"He didn't say what his name was." She took my hand. "But now I've read you, now you can—"

I pulled free. "What did he look like?"

"Wow, you really *are* scared."

"What did he look like?"

"Why's it so important?"

"Please, Anita."

"Okay, okay, take it easy. Thin man. Nazi fringe. Handsome. Had a long nail on his index finger."

Shit. *The Fisherman always finds what he's looking for. You and I may not know how, but he knows. Always.*

I swallowed. "When did you see him?"

"Just before you arrived. He went up into the village, said he was going to talk to someone."

"What did he want?"

"He was looking for some southerner called Jon. Is that you?"

I shook my head. "My name's Ulf. What else did he say?"

"Nothing. He gave me his phone number in case I heard anything, but it was an Oslo number. Why are you going on about it?"

"I'm just waiting for someone to show up with my shotgun, but it probably isn't him."

So Johnny Moe was here. And I had left the pistol in the cabin. I'd gone somewhere I wasn't safe, and I hadn't taken the only thing that might make me a bit safer. Because I thought it might be tricky if I met a woman and had to get undressed. And now I had met a woman, and evidently didn't want to get undressed after all. Is there a level *below* idiot? The funny thing was that I was more annoyed than frightened. I should have been more scared. He had come to shoot me. I was hiding here because I wanted to survive, wasn't I? So I'd better get my fucking act together and do a bit of surviving!

"You live behind the church, you said?"

She brightened up. "Yes, it's not far."

I looked up at the gravel track. He could come back anytime. "Can we take a detour through the church-yard, so that no one sees us?"

"Why don't you want anyone to see us?"

"Just thinking about . . . er, your reputation."

"My reputation?" She snorted. "Everyone knows that Anita likes men."

"Okay, mine, then."

She shrugged. "Okay, if you're so bloody precious."

The house had curtains.

And a pair of man's shoes in the passage.

"Whose . . . ?"

"My father's," Anita said. "And you don't have to whisper, he's asleep."

"Isn't that when people normally whisper?"

"Still scared?"

I looked at the shoes. They were smaller than mine. "No."

"Good. Come on."

We went into her bedroom. It was cramped, and the bed was only meant for one person. One thin person. She pulled her dress over her head, unbuttoned my trousers, then pulled them and my underpants down with one tug. Then she unhooked her bra and slipped her pants off. Her skin was pale, almost white, with red marks and scratches here and there. But no needle tracks. She was nice. It wasn't that.

She sat down on the bed and looked up at me. "You might as well take your jacket off."

While I was taking off my jacket, and hanging it and my shirt on the only chair in there, I heard snoring from the next room. Harsh, grating breaths in, spluttering breaths out, like a broken silencer. She opened the bedside cabinet.

"No condoms left," she said. "You'll have to be careful, because I don't want a kid."

"I'm no good at being careful," I said quickly. "Never have been. Maybe we could just ... er, play around a bit?"

"Play around?" She uttered the words as though they disgusted her. "Dad's got condoms."

She left the room naked and I heard the door to the next room open; the snoring stuttered a bit before carrying on as before. A few seconds later she was back with a worn brown wallet which she was searching through.

"Here," she said, tossing a little square of plastic at me.

The plastic was frayed at the edges. I looked for an expiry date, but couldn't find one.

"I can't do it with a condom," I said. "It just doesn't work."

"Yes, it will," she said, grabbing hold of my terrified cock.

"Sorry. So what do you do here in Kåsund, Anita?"

"Shut up."

"Hmm. Maybe it needs a bit of . . . er, iodine?"

"I said shut up."

I looked down at the little hand which evidently believed it could work miracles. I wondered where Johnny could be. In such a small village it wouldn't be difficult to find someone able to tell him that the recently arrived southerner was staying in the hunting cabin. He would look there and at the wedding party. Kornelius had promised to keep quiet. As long as I stayed where I was, I was safe.

"There, see!" Anita chirruped happily.

I looked down at the miracle, astonished. It had to be some sort of stress reaction—I've read that hanged men sometimes get erections. Without letting go or stopping, she picked up the condom packet with her left hand, tore it open with her teeth, sucked out the condom and formed a circle around it with her lips. Then she dived down, and when she lifted her head again I was equipped and ready for battle. She leaned back on the bed and spread her legs.

"I just want to say that—"

"Haven't you finished talking yet, Ulf?"

"I don't like being thrown out immediately afterwards. It's all to do with self-respect, if you—"

"Just shut up and get going while you still can."

"You promise?"

She sighed. "Just fuck me."

I crawled up onto the bed. She helped me into place. I closed my eyes and started to thrust, not too fast, not too slow. She groaned, cursed and swore, but in a way I found encouraging. In the absence of any other metronome, I fell into the same rhythm as the snoring in the next room. I could feel it building. I tried not to think about the state of the condom, or what a combination of Anita and me would look like.

Suddenly she stiffened and stopped making any noise at all.

I stopped thrusting. I thought she'd heard something, some irregularity in her father's snoring, or someone approaching the house. I held my breath and listened. To my ears the jagged snoring sounded just the same as before.

Then the body beneath me suddenly went completely limp. I looked down at her anxiously. Her eyes were closed and she looked lifeless. Carefully I put my thumb and forefinger to her throat, feeling for a pulse. I couldn't find it. Fuck, where was the pulse, was she . . . ?

Then a low sound emerged from her mouth. First a dull growl, which got louder. And turned into something very familiar. Grating breaths in, breaths out like a broken silencer.

Yep, she was her father's daughter.

I squeezed in between the slim female form and the wall, and felt the cold wallpaper behind my back and the bed-frame against my hip. But I was safe. For the time being.

I closed my eyes. Two thoughts struck me. That the thought of Valium *hadn't* struck me. And *you're going to shoot the reflection.*

Then I drifted off into dreamland.

CHAPTER 9

When I saw Anita's father at the breakfast table, he was a pretty good match for what I'd imagined based on the sound of his snoring. Hairy, rather fat, and gruff. I even imagined that I'd somehow heard his string vest in his snoring.

"All right?" he said. Gruffly. And stubbed out his cigarette on the half-eaten slice of bread in front of him. "You look like you need coffee."

"Thanks," I said, relieved, and sat down opposite him at the folding table.

He looked at me. Then he turned back to his newspaper, licked the end of his pencil, and nodded towards the stove and kettle. "Get it yourself. You don't get to fuck my daughter and have coffee served to you."

I nodded and found a cup in the cupboard. I filled it with pitch-black coffee as I peered out through the window. Still overcast.

Anita's father stared down at the newspaper. In the silence I could hear her snoring.

My watch said quarter past nine. Was Johnny still in the village, or had he moved on to look somewhere else?

I took a sip of the coffee. I almost felt I ought to chew it before swallowing.

"Give me"—the man looked up at me—"another word for 'castration.' "

I looked back at him. "Sterilisation."

He looked down at the paper. Counted. "With one *r*?"

"Yes."

"Okay, maybe." He licked the pencil and filled in the word.

While I was putting my shoes on in the passageway and was about to leave, Anita came storming out of her bedroom. Pale and naked, hair all over the place, wild-eyed. She wrapped her arms round me, holding me tight.

"I didn't want to wake you," I said, and tried in vain to reach the door.

"Will you come back?"

I leaned back and looked at her. She knew that I knew. That they didn't usually come back. But still she wanted to know. Or not.

"I'll try," I said.

"Try?"

"Yes."

"Look at me. *Look* at me! You promise?"

"Of course."

"There, you said it, Ulf. You *promised.* And no one makes a promise to Anita without keeping it. I've got a stake in your soul now."

I gulped. Nodded. To be strictly accurate, I hadn't promised to do anything but try. Try to want to, try to find time, for instance. I pulled one arm free and reached for the door handle.

I walked back to the cabin the long way. I went round the hills to the northeast so I could approach through the clump of woodland. I crept closer through the trees.

The buck was marking its territory by rubbing one horn against the corner of the cabin. It wouldn't dare do that if there was anyone inside. Even so, I slipped down into the furrow carved out by the stream and followed it at a crouch to the place where I had hidden the rifle. I removed the stones, unrolled the rifle from the roofing felt, checked it was loaded, and walked quickly towards the cabin.

The buck remained where it was, looking at me with interest. God knows what it could smell. I went inside.

Someone had been there.

Johnny had been there.

I glanced round the room. Not much had changed. The cupboard door was ajar, and I always made sure I closed it properly because of the mice. The empty leather case was sticking out slightly from beneath the bunk bed, and there was ash on the inside door handle. I removed the plank next to the cupboard and stuck my arm in. I let out a sigh of relief as I felt the pistol and money belt. Then I sat down on one of the chairs and tried to work out what he might have been thinking.

The case told him I had been there. But the fact that there was no money, dope or any other personal possessions in sight might suggest to him that I had left, having got hold of a more practical rucksack or something. Then he had stuck his hand into the ash in the wood-burning stove to see if it was still warm, to get an idea of what sort of head start I might have.

That was as far as I could follow his reasoning. What next? Would he have moved on somewhere else if he had no idea of where I might have gone, or why I had left Kåsund? Or was he hiding somewhere nearby, waiting for me to come back? But if that was the case, wouldn't he have taken more care to cover his tracks, so that I wouldn't suspect anything? Or—hang on—here I was, thinking that the obvious signs of his visit meant he had moved on—and what if that was exactly what he wanted me to think!

Fuck.

I grabbed the binoculars and scanned the horizon, which I now knew down to the smallest detail. Looking for someone, or something, that hadn't been there before. Staring. Concentrating.

I did it again.

After an hour or so I started to feel tired. But I didn't want to make coffee and have the smoke signal that I was back to anyone within several kilometres.

If only it would start to rain, if only those clouds would drop their load, if only something would *happen*. This damn waiting was driving me mad.

I put the binoculars down. Closed my eyes for a moment.

I walked out to the reindeer.

It looked at me warily, but didn't move.

I stroked its antlers.

Then I climbed up onto its back.

"Giddy up," I said.

It took a few steps. Hesitantly at first.

"Yes!"

Then more firmly. Then faster. Towards the village. Its knees clicked, faster and faster, like a Geiger counter approaching an atom bomb.

The church was burned out. Obviously the Germans had been there. Hunting for members of the resistance. But the ruins were still standing, warm and smouldering. Stone and ash. And around the black stones they were dancing, some of them naked. They were dancing incredibly fast, even if the priest's singing was slow and laboured. His white cassock was black with soot, and in front of him stood the bridal couple, her dressed in black, him in white, from his white cap to his white wooden shoes. The singing died away, and I rode closer.

"In the name of the Norwegian state, I pronounce you man and wife," he said, then spat brown saliva on the crucifix hanging next to him, raised a judge's gavel and struck the charred black altar rail. Once. Twice. Three times.

I woke up with a start. I was sitting with my head against the wall. Damn, these dreams were wearing me out.

But the banging was still audible.

My heart stopped beating, and I stared at the door.

The rifle was leaning against the wall.

I grabbed it without getting up from the chair. I put the butt against my shoulder and rested my cheek against the side of it. My finger on the trigger. I let out the breath I realised I had been holding.

Two more bangs.

Then the door opened.

The sky had cleared. And it was evening. Because the door faced west, the figure in the doorway had the sun behind it, so all I could see was a dark silhouette with a halo of orange light, against the low hills.

"Are you going to shoot me?"

"Sorry," I said, lowering the rifle. "I thought it was a grouse."

Her laughter was deep and genuine, but her face was in shadow, so I could only imagine the shimmering light in her eyes.

CHAPTER 10

Johnny had gone.

"He caught the bus back south today," Lea said.

She had sent Knut out of the cabin to get wood and water. She wanted coffee. And an explanation as to why she had received a visit from a southerner who wanted to know where I was.

I shrugged. "There are lots of southerners. So what did he want?"

"He said he'd really like to talk to you. About business."

"Oh, right," I said. "Was it Johnny? Looks like a wading bird?"

She didn't answer, just sat there on the other side of the table and tried to catch my eye.

"He'd found out that you were staying in the hunting cabin, and got someone to show him the way. But you weren't here, and then when someone else told him you'd been at mine after the funeral, I suppose he thought I might know something."

"And what did you say?"

I let her catch my eye. Let her study my expression. I had plenty to hide, yet also nothing.

She sighed: "I said you'd gone back south."

"Why did you say that?"

"Because I'm not stupid. I don't know what sort of trouble you're in, and I don't want to know, but I don't want to be responsible for things getting even worse."

"*Even* worse?"

She shook her head. That could mean that she'd expressed herself badly, that I had misunderstood, or that she didn't want to talk about it. She glanced out through one of the window slits. We could hear Knut chopping wood energetically outside.

"According to him, your name is Jon, not Ulf."

"Did you ever believe it was Ulf?"

"No."

"But you still sent him off in the wrong direction. You lied. What does your book say about that?"

She nodded in the direction of the chopping. "He says we need to look after you. The book has something to say about that as well."

We sat in silence for a while. Me with my hands on the table, she with hers in her lap.

"Thanks for taking care of Knut after the funeral."

"Don't mention it. How is he taking it?"

"Well, really."

"And you?"

She shrugged her shoulders. "Women always find a way of coping."

The chopping had stopped. He'd soon be back. She looked at me again. Her eyes had taken on a colour I'd never seen before, and the look in them had a corrosive intensity. "I've changed my mind. I want to know what you're running from."

"Your original decision was probably more sensible."

"Tell me."

"What for?"

"Because I believe you're a good person. And good people's sins can always be forgiven."

"What if you're wrong, what if I'm not a good person? Does that mean I'd end up burning in that hell of yours?" It came out more bitterly than I intended.

"I'm not wrong, Ulf, because I can see you. I can see you."

I took a deep breath. I still didn't know if the words

were going to come out of my mouth. I was inside her eyes, blue, blue as the sea below you when you're ten years old and standing on a rock and your whole being wants to jump, apart from your legs, which won't move.

"I had a job that involved chasing drug-related debts and killing people," I heard myself say. "I stole money from my employer, and now he's hunting me. And I've managed to get Knut, your ten-year-old son, involved in this as well. I'm paying him to spy for me. Well, not even that—he gets paid if he can report anything suspicious. For instance, if he sees the sort of people who wouldn't hesitate to kill a young boy if it was necessary." I shook a cigarette out of the packet. "How am I doing on forgiveness now?"

She opened her mouth just as Knut opened the door.

"There," he said, dropping the wood on the floor in front of the stove. "I'm starving now."

Lea looked at me.

"I've got tinned fish balls," I said.

"Yuck," Knut said. "Can't we have fresh cod instead?"

"I'm afraid I haven't got any."

"Not here. In the sea. We can go fishing. Can we, Mum?"

"It's the middle of the night," she said quietly. She was still staring at me.

"That's the best time to go fishing," Knut said, jumping up and down. "Please, Mum!"

"We haven't got a boat, Knut."

It took a moment for him to realise what she meant. I looked at Knut. His face darkened. Then he brightened up again. "We can take Grandpa's boat. It's in the boathouse, he said I could."

"Did he?"

"Yes! Cod! Cod! You like cod, don't you, Ulf?"

"I love cod," I said, meeting her gaze. "But I don't know if your mother wants any right now."

"Yes, she does, don't you, Mum?"

She didn't answer.

"Mum?"

"We'll let Ulf decide," she said.

The boy squeezed between the table and my chair, forcing me to look at him.

"Ulf?"

"Yes, Knut?"

"You can have the tongue."

The boathouse lay some hundred metres from the jetty. The smell of rotten seaweed and salt water stirred some vague summer memories into life. Something about having my head poked through a life jacket that was too small, a cousin showing off because they were rich enough to have a boat *and* a cabin, and a red-faced uncle swearing because he couldn't get the outboard motor started.

It was dark inside the boathouse, and there was a pleasant smell of tar. Everything we needed for fishing was already in the boat, its keel held in a wooden cradle.

"Isn't that a bit big for a rowing boat?" I estimated that it was five or six metres long.

"Oh, it's no more than medium-sized," Lea said. "Come on, we've all got to push."

"Dad's was much bigger," Knut said. "A ten-oared boat, with a mast."

We launched the boat, and I managed to clamber in without getting my legs too wet.

I fitted the oars in place on one of the two pairs of rowlocks, and began to row out away from shore with calm, strong strokes. I recalled putting a lot of effort into being better at rowing than my cousin during the one summer that I, poor, fatherless relation, was allowed to be a guest there. Even so, I thought I could see that Lea and Knut weren't impressed.

Some way out I pulled the oars in.

Knut crept towards the back of the boat, leaned over the gunwale, threw the line out and stared after it. I could see the distant look in his eyes as his imagination roamed free.

"Good lad," I said, taking off the jacket that had been hanging on a hook in the boathouse.

She nodded.

There was no wind, and the sea—or ocean, as Lea and Knut called it—was shiny as a mirror. It looked solid enough for us to walk towards the red cauldron of the sun sticking above the horizon off to the north.

"Knut said you haven't got anyone waiting for you back home," she said.

I shook my head. "Fortunately not."

"That must be strange."

"What?"

"Not having anyone. No one thinking of you. No one looking after you. Or no one to look after."

"I've tried," I said, loosening the hook from one of the lines. "And I couldn't handle it."

"You couldn't handle having a family?"

"I couldn't handle looking after them," I said. "I'm—as you must have realised by now—not the sort of man you can rely on."

"I hear you say that, Ulf, but I don't know if it's true. What happened?"

I pulled the spoon bait free from the line. "Why are you still calling me Ulf?"

"That's what you told me your name was, so that's the name I use. Until you want to be called something different. Everyone should be allowed to change their name every so often."

"And how long have you been called Lea?"

She screwed one eye up. "Are you asking a woman how old she is?"

"I didn't mean . . ."

"Twenty-nine years."

"Hmm. Lea's a nice name, no reason to change—"

"It means 'cow,'" she interrupted. "I'd like to be called Sara. That means 'princess.' But my father said I couldn't be called Sara Sara. So instead I've been called cow for twenty-nine years. What do you have to say about that?"

"Well." I thought for a moment. "Moo?"

At first she looked at me in disbelief. Then she started to laugh. That deep laugh. Slow guffaws. Knut turned round in the stern. "What is it? Did he tell a joke?"

"Yes," she said, without taking her eyes off me. "I think he did."

"Tell me!"

"Later." She leaned towards me. "So, what happened?"

"I don't know that anything happened." I cast the line out. "I was just too late."

She frowned. "Too late for what?"

"To save my daughter." The water was so clear

that I could see the shimmering spoon lure sink deeper and deeper. Until it vanished out of sight in the greenish black darkness. "When I finally had the money she was already in a coma. She died three weeks after I had scraped together the cost of the treatment in Germany. Not that it would have made any difference—it was already too late. At least that's what the doctors said. But the point is that I couldn't do what I was supposed to. I let her down. That's been the constant refrain to my life. But the fact that I couldn't handle ... that I couldn't even manage when . . ."

I sniffed. Maybe I shouldn't have taken the jacket off; after all, we were close to the North Pole. I felt something on my lower arm. My hair stood on end. A touch. I couldn't remember the last time a woman had touched me. Until I remembered that it was less than twenty-four hours ago. To hell with this place, these people, all this.

"That was why you stole the money, wasn't it?"

I shrugged.

"You stole the money for your daughter, even though you knew they'd kill you if they got hold of you."

I spat over the side of the boat to see something break the terrible stillness of the water. "It sounds good when you put it like that," I said. "Let's just say

I was a father who waited until it was too late to do anything for his daughter."

"But it was already too late, wasn't it, according to the doctors?"

"They said so, but they didn't *know*. No one *knows*. Not me, not you, not the priest, not the atheist. So we believe. Believe, because that's better than realising that there's only one thing waiting for us down in the depths, and that's darkness, cold. Death."

"Do you really believe that?"

"Do you really believe there's a pearly gate with angels and a bloke called St. Peter? Actually, no, you don't believe that—a sect about ten thousand times bigger than yours believes in saints. And they think that if you don't believe precisely what they believe in, down to the smallest detail, then you'll end up in hell. Yep, Catholics believe that you Lutherans are heading straight down to the basement. And you believe that's where they're going. You really were pretty lucky being born among true believers up here near the North Pole instead of in Italy or Spain. Then you'd have had a very long road to salvation."

I saw the line go slack, and pulled at it. It jerked, apparently caught on something; it must be shallow here. I tugged harder and the line came free of whatever it was caught on.

"You're angry, Ulf."

"Angry? I'm fucking furious, that's what I am.

If that god of yours exists, why does he play with humanity like that, why does he let one person be born into suffering and another into a life of excess, or one with a chance of finding the faith that's supposed to save them, while the majority never get to hear a thing about God. Why would he . . . how could he . . . ?"

Damn cold.

"Take your daughter?" she asked quietly.

I blinked. "There's nothing down there," I said. "Just darkness, death, and—"

"Fish!" Knut cried.

We turned towards him. He was already hauling in the line. Lea patted my arm one last time, then let go of me and leaned against the gunwale.

We stared down into the water. Waiting for whatever he had caught to come into view. For some reason I found myself thinking of a yellow sou'wester. And suddenly I had a premonition. No, it was more than a premonition. I knew for certain: he would come back. I closed my eyes. Yes, I could see it quite clearly. Johnny would come back. He knew I was still here.

"Ha!" Knut said jubilantly.

When I opened my eyes, a large cod was wriggling in the bottom of the boat. Its eyes were bulging, as if it couldn't believe what it was seeing. Which was fair enough—this could hardly have been how it thought things would turn out.

CHAPTER 11

We rowed to an island where the keel scraped softly against the sand. It was only a couple of hundred metres between the gently rounded island and the mainland, which tumbled abruptly and darkly into the sea from the heather-covered plateau. Knut took his shoes off, waded ashore and tied the boat to a rock. I offered to carry Lea, but she just smiled and made me the same offer.

Knut and I made a fire and lit it while Lea gutted and cleaned the fish.

"Once we caught so many fish that we had to fetch the wheelbarrow to empty the boat," Knut said. He was already licking his lips.

I couldn't ever remember being that fond of fish when I was a boy. Maybe that's because it was mostly served in the form of deep-fried fritters or fish fingers, or shaped into balls in a white, semen-like sauce.

"There's a lot of food here," Lea said, wrapping the entire fish in silver foil and placing it directly on the flames. "Ten minutes."

Knut clambered onto my back, clearly excited at the prospect of food. "Wrestling match!" he cried, clinging onto me even when I tried to stand up. "The southerner must die!"

"There's a mosquito on my back," I yelled, and bucked, tossing him back and forth like a rodeo rider until he landed on the sand with a happy yelp.

"If we're going to wrestle, we'd better do it properly," I said.

"Yes! What's properly?"

"Sumo wrestling," I said, then picked up a stick and drew a circle in the fine sand. "First one to make the other person step outside the circle wins."

I showed him the ceremony that preceded each bout, and how we should squat opposite each other outside the circle and clap our hands once.

"That's a prayer for the gods to be with us in the fight, so we aren't alone."

I saw Lea frown, but she didn't say anything.

The boy followed my actions as I slowly raised my palms, looked down, and then put them on my knees.

"That's to crush evil spirits," I said, then stamped my feet.

Knut did the same.

"Ready . . . steady . . ." I whispered.

Knut twisted his face into an aggressive grimace.

"Go!"

He leaped into the circle and tackled me with his shoulder.

"You're out!" he declared triumphantly.

My footprint outside the circle left no room for doubt. Lea laughed and clapped.

"It's not over yet, *rikishi* Knut-*san* from Finnmark *ken*," I snarled, and squatted down again. "First to five is Futabayama."

"Futa . . . ?" Knut quickly crouched down on the other side.

"Futabayama. Sumo legend. Big fat bastard. Ready . . . steady . . ."

I got him in a body lock that carried him well outside the circle.

When the score was 4–4, Knut was so sweaty and wound up that he forgot the preliminaries and hurled himself at me. I stepped aside. He couldn't stop in time, and stumbled outside the circle.

Lea laughed. Knut lay there motionless with his head in the sand.

I sat down next to him.

"In sumo, some things are more important than

winning," I said. "Like showing dignity in both victory and defeat."

"I lost," Knut whispered into the sand. "I expect it's easier to do that when you win."

"It is."

"Well, congratulations. You're Futa . . . Futa . . ."

". . . bayama. And Futabayama salutes you, courageous Haguroyama."

He raised his head. He had sand stuck to his wet face. "Who's that?"

"Futabayama's apprentice. Haguroyama also went on to be a master."

"Did he? He beat Futabayama?"

"Oh, yes. Toyed with him. He just had to learn a few things first. Such as how to lose."

Knut sat up. He squinted at me. "Does losing make you better, Ulf?"

I nodded slowly. I saw that Lea was paying attention too. "You get better"—I squashed a midge that had landed on my arm—"at losing."

"Better at losing? Is there any point in being good at that?"

"Life is mostly about trying things you can't do," I said. "You end up losing more often than you win. Even Futabayama kept on losing before he started to win. And it's important to be good at something you're going to do more often, isn't it?"

"I suppose so." He thought about it. "But what does being good at losing actually mean?"

I met Lea's gaze over the boy's shoulder. "Daring to lose again," I said.

"Food's ready," she replied.

The skin of the cod had stuck to the silver foil, so when Lea opened the parcel up, we just had to pull off pieces of the white flesh and pop them in our mouths.

"Heavenly," I said. I didn't know what I meant by *heavenly*, but I couldn't think of a better word.

"Mmm," Knut purred.

"All we're missing is the white wine," I said.

"Burn," he said, flashing his teeth.

"Jesus drank wine," Lea said. "Anyway, you drink red wine with cod." She laughed as Knut and I both stopped eating and looked at her. "Or so I've heard!"

"Dad used to drink," Knut said.

Lea stopped laughing.

"More wrestling!" Knut said.

I patted my stomach to show that I was too full.

"Boring . . ." His bottom lip drooped.

"See if you can find any gulls' eggs," Lea said.

"Eggs, now?" Knut asked.

"Summer eggs," she said. "They're rare, but they do exist."

He closed one eye. Then he stood up, raced off and disappeared over the brow of the island.

"Summer eggs?" I asked, lying back on the sand. "Is that true?"

"I think most things exist," she said. "And I did say they were rare."

"Like your lot?"

"Us?"

"Læstadians."

"Is that how you see us?" She shaded her eyes, and I realised where Knut had picked up his habit of squinting with one eye.

"No," I said eventually, and closed both eyes.

"Tell me something, Ulf." She put the jacket I had borrowed under her head.

"What?"

"Anything."

"Let me think."

We lay in silence. I listened to the fire crackle and the waves play gently on the shore.

"A summer's night in Stockholm," I said. "Everything's green. Everyone is asleep. I'm walking slowly home with Monica. We stop and kiss. And then we carry on. We hear laughter from an open window. There's a breeze coming from the archipelago, carrying with it a smell of grass and seaweed." I hummed inside my head. "And the breeze strokes our cheeks and I pull her closer to me, and the night doesn't exist, only stillness, shadow, wind."

"That's lovely," she said. "Go on."

"The night is short and light and slips away as the thrushes wake up. A man stops rowing to look at a swan. As we walk across the Western Bridge, a single, empty tram passes us. And there, in the middle of the night, in secret, the trees blossom in Stockholm as the windows paint the city with light. And the city plays a song for everyone who's sleeping, for everyone who has to travel far away but will come back to Stockholm again. The streets are scented with flowers, and we kiss again, and walk slowly, slowly home through the city."

I listened. Waves. Fire. A distant gull's cry.

"Monica, is she your beloved?"

"Yes," I said. "She's my beloved."

"Ah. How long?"

"Let's see. Ten years or so, I think."

"That's a long time."

"Yes, but we're only ever in love for three minutes at a time."

"Three minutes?"

"Three minutes and nineteen seconds, to be more precise. That's how long it takes her to sing the song."

I heard her sit up. "What you just told me is a song?"

"'Slowly We Walk Through the City,'" I said. "Monica Zetterlund."

"And you've never met her?"

"No. I had a ticket to see her and Steve Kuhn in concert in Stockholm, but then Anna got ill and I had to work."

She nodded silently.

"It must be nice to be so happy with someone," she said. "Like the couple in the song, I mean."

"But it doesn't last."

"You don't know that."

"True. No one knows. But, in your experience, does it last?"

There was a sudden cold gust, and I opened my eyes. Saw something on the edge of the cliff on the other side of the water. Probably the silhouette of a big rock. I turned towards Lea. She was sitting hunched up.

"I'm just saying that everything could exist," she said. "Even eternal love."

Strands of hair were blowing into her face, and it struck me that she had it. That same blue shimmer. Unless it was just the light out here.

"Sorry, it's none of my business, I just ..." I stopped. My eyes searched for the rock, but couldn't find it again.

"You just ..."

I took a deep breath. Knew I'd regret this. "I was

standing under the window of the workroom after the funeral. I overheard you talking to your husband's brother."

She folded her arms. Looked at me. Not shocked, but studious. She glanced in the direction Knut had disappeared in, then looked at me again.

"I have no experience of how long love for a man can last, because I never loved the man I was given."

"Given? Are you saying it was an arranged marriage?"

She shook her head. "Arranged marriages are what families used to organise between them in the olden days. Favourable alliances. Grazing pasture and herds of reindeer. The same faith. Hugo and I didn't have that sort of marriage."

"So?"

"It was a forced marriage."

"Who forced you?"

"Circumstances." She looked round for Knut again.

"You were . . . ?"

"Yes, I was pregnant."

"I appreciate that your religion isn't particularly tolerant of children outside marriage, but Hugo wasn't from a Læstadian family, was he?"

She shook her head. "Circumstances, and Father. Those two things forced us into it. He said he'd expel me from the congregation if I didn't do as he commanded. Expulsion means not having anyone, being *completely* alone. Do you understand?" She put her hand to her mouth. At first I thought it was to cover her scar. "I've seen what happens to people who get expelled . . ."

"I get it . . ."

"No, you *don't* get it, Ulf. And I don't know why I'm telling all this to a stranger." Only now did I hear the sob in her voice.

"Perhaps precisely because I am a stranger."

"Yes, perhaps," she sniffed. "You're going to leave."

"How could your father force Hugo when Hugo wasn't part of a congregation he could be expelled from?"

"Father told him that if he didn't marry me, he'd report him for raping me."

I looked at her in silence.

She sat up, straightened her back, lifted her head, and looked out to sea.

"Yes, I married the man who raped me when I was eighteen years old. And had his child."

There was a shrill shriek from the mainland. I turned. A black cormorant was flying close over the water below the cliff.

"Because that's your interpretation of the Bible?"

"In our home there's only one person who interprets the Word."

"Your father."

She shrugged. "I went home the night it happened, and told Mother that Hugo had raped me. She comforted me, but said it was best to let it go. Getting one of Eliassen's sons convicted for rape, what good would that do? But when she realised I was pregnant she went to Father. His first reaction was to ask if we had prayed to God that I wouldn't get pregnant. His second was that Hugo and I must get married."

She swallowed. Paused. And I realised this was something she had told very few people. Perhaps no one at all. That I offered the first and best opportunity for her to say these things out loud after the funeral.

"Then he went to see old Eliassen," she went on. "Hugo's father and my father are powerful men here in the village, in their different ways. Old Eliassen gives people work at sea, and my father gives them the Word and eases their troubled souls. Father said that if Eliassen didn't agree, he'd have no problem persuading someone in his congregation that they'd seen and heard a thing or two that night. Old Eliassen replied that Father didn't have to threaten him, that I was a good match regardless, and maybe I could calm Hugo down a bit. And once the two of them had decided that was what was going to happen, that was what happened."

"How—" I began, but was interrupted by another shriek. This time not a bird.

Knut.

We both leaped to our feet.

The Fisherman always finds what he's looking for.

Another scream. We ran towards it. I reached the top of the island first. Saw him. I turned to Lea, who was running behind me with her skirt pulled up.

"He's all right."

The boy was standing about a hundred metres away from us, staring at something on the shore.

"What is it?" I called down to him.

He pointed at something black that the waves were lapping over. And then I picked up the smell. The smell of a corpse.

"What is it?" Lea asked as she arrived beside me.

I did the same as Knut, and pointed.

"Death and destruction," she said.

I held her back when she made to go down to Knut. "Maybe you should stay here, and I'll go and see what it is."

"No need," she said. "I can see what it is."

"So . . . what is it?"

"A pup."

"A pup?"

"A young seal," she said. "A dead one."

It was still night as we rowed back.

It was completely calm: all you could hear was the

splash of the oars as they left the water, the drops sparkling like diamonds as they fell in the slanting sunlight.

I was sitting in the back of the boat, watching mother and son row. I was humming "Slowly We Walk Through the City" inside my head. They were like a single organism. Knut—with a look of deep concentration—was trying to keep his body firm, using his back and hips, and maintaining a calm, even, adult rhythm with the heavy oars. His mother was sitting behind him, matching his movements, taking care to synchronise their strokes. No one said anything. The veins and sinews on the backs of her hands moved and her black hair blew to one side as she turned to look over her shoulder every now and then to make sure our course was correct. Of course Knut was trying to make out that he wasn't hoping to impress me with his rowing, but kept giving himself away by taking sneaky glances at me. I pushed my jaw out and nodded appreciatively. He pretended not to notice, but I could see him put a bit more effort into his strokes.

We used a rope fastened to a pulley to drag the boat onto the wooden cradle and into the boathouse. It was surprisingly easy to pull the heavy boat up. I couldn't help thinking about mankind's persistent inventiveness and capacity to survive. And our willingness to do terrible things if need be.

We walked along the gravel road towards the houses. Stopped at the telephone pole at the start of the path. A fresh layer of posters had been stuck on top of the dance-band advertisement.

"Goodbye, Ulf," she said. "I've enjoyed spending time with you. Get home safely, and sleep well."

"Goodbye," I said, and smiled. They really did take their farewells very seriously up here. Maybe it was because the distances were so great, and the surroundings so brutal. You couldn't take it for granted you'd see each other again soon. Or at all.

"And we'd be very happy to see you at the prayer meeting in the parish house on Saturday morning." She said this in a slightly stiff tone of voice, and her face twitched. "Wouldn't we, Knut?"

Knut nodded, mute and already half asleep.

"Thanks, but I think it's probably too late for me to be saved." I don't know if the ambiguity was intentional.

"It can't do any harm to hear the Word." She looked at me with those strange, intense eyes that always seemed to be searching for something.

"On one condition," I said. "That I can borrow your car and drive to Alta afterwards. I need to buy a couple of things."

"Can you drive?"

I shrugged.

"Maybe I could come too," she said.

"You don't have to."

"She's not as easy as she looks."

I don't know if the ambiguity was intentional.

When I got to the cabin I lay down and fell asleep straight away without touching the bottle of drink. As far as I can remember, I didn't dream. And I woke up with a sense that something had happened. Something good. And it had been a hell of a long time since that last happened to me.

CHAPTER 12

Holy Spirit, to Thee we pray
That we in the one true faith might stay,
And help defend it with all our heart
Until our final breath,
When we from earthly misery depart
For home with Thee upon our death
Kyrie eleison!

The hymn rolled like slow thunder around the walls of the little prayer hall. It sounded as though the whole congregation, all twenty-something of them, were joining in.

I tried to follow the words in the little black book

Lea had handed me. Landstad's hymnbook. "Authorised by royal resolution, 1869," it said on the title page. I'd already leafed through it. Didn't look as though a single syllable had been altered since then.

When the hymn was over, a man walked with heavy steps across the creaking wooden floor to a simple lectern. He turned towards us.

It was Lea's father. Grandpa. Jakob Sara.

"*I believe in God the Father, the Almighty, Creator of Heaven and Earth,*" he began. All the others remained silent, and let him read out the whole declaration of faith alone. Afterwards he remained motionless, silently staring down at the lectern. For a long time. Just as I was convinced something was wrong, that he was suffering some kind of mental block, he raised his voice:

"Dear Christians. In the name of the Father, the Son and the Holy Spirit. Yes, we wanted to start this meeting in the name of the Holy Trinity. Yes." Another pause. He was still standing with his head bowed, huddled in a suit that was slightly too big for him, like a nervous beginner, and certainly not the hardened, well-travelled preacher Knut had talked about. "For if one is to look at oneself, one's own being, it is not good to step up to this pulpit as a wretched sinner." Stop. I glanced around. Oddly enough, no one else seemed to feel at all uncomfortable with the man's obvious struggle. I managed to count to ten before he went on: "And this valuable thing we are gathered here for, the holy, pure Word of God—one must ask, how can this word be upheld? That is, why is it so difficult to step up to this lectern, because what is one to do?" He finally raised his head. Looked straight at us. There was no trace of uncertainty in his firm, direct gaze. No sign of the humility he claimed to be afflicted by. "For we are naught but dust. And to dust we shall return. But we shall have eternal life if we remain true to the faith. This world in which we live is a world in decay, governed by the Ruler of the World, the Devil, Satan, he who seduces the flock." I couldn't swear to it, but wasn't he looking straight at me? "In this world we poor wretches must live. If we can forsake the Devil, and can spend the brief time that remains walking in hope."

Another hymn. Lea and I were sitting closest to the exit, and I signalled to her that I was going outside for a cigarette.

Outside the meeting house I leaned against the wall and listened to the singing inside.

"Forgive me asking, but could I have one of your coffin nails?"

The meeting house lay at the end of the road. Mattis must have been waiting round the corner. I offered him the packet.

"Have they managed to save you?" he asked.

"Not yet," I said. "Their singing's a bit too out of tune."

He laughed. "Oh, you have to learn how to hear the hymns the right way. Singing carefully in tune, that's the sort of thing worldly people think is important. But for true believers, emotion is everything. Why else do you think we Sámi became Læstadians? Believe me, Ulf, it's only a stone's throw from the drumming of a shaman and witchcraft to the Læstadians' speaking in tongues, healing and emotionalism." I gave him a light. "And this infernal, ponderous hymn-singing . . ." he muttered.

We took a synchronised drag on our cigarettes and listened. When they had finished Lea's father began to speak again.

"Is the preacher supposed to sound like he's suffering up there?" I asked.

"What, Jakob Sara? Yes. His job is to make out that he's just a foolish Christian who hasn't actually chosen to stand in the pulpit but has been chosen by the church." Mattis bowed his head and made his voice as deep as the preacher's: *"My desire since I was chosen to lead this congregation has always been for God to bend me to obedience. But one is burdened by one's own corrupt flesh."* He took a drag on his cigarette. "That's how it's been for a hundred years. The ideal is humility and simplicity."

"Your cousin told me you were one of them."

"But then I saw the light," Mattis said, and looked at the cigarette with displeasure. "Tell me, is there actually any tobacco in this?"

"You stopped believing when you were studying theology?"

"Yes, but up here they counted me as lost the moment I set off for Oslo. A true Læstadian doesn't study to become a priest among worldly folk. Here the preacher's only task is to impart the old, true creed, not new-fangled rubbish from Oslo."

The latest hymn had come to an end inside, and Jakob Sara's voice rang out again:

"The Lord is long-suffering, but have no doubt, he will come like a thief in the night, and the elements and the earth shall fall apart when that lack of faith is revealed."

"Speaking of which," Mattis said, "those of us living under a death sentence don't want him to come any sooner than he has to, do we?"

"Sorry?"

"I daresay some people would be very happy if they never saw him in Kåsund again."

I stopped mid-drag.

"Okay," Mattis said. "I don't know if that Johnny went further north or headed home, but the fact that he didn't find what he was looking for is no guarantee that he won't come back."

I coughed out some smoke.

"He won't come back straight away, of course. No, you're probably safe there, Ulf. But someone might decide to dial a number and say a few words over those." He pointed at the telephone wires above our heads. "They could have been promised money for it."

I threw my cigarette on the ground. "Are you going to tell me why you came here, Mattis?"

"He said you'd taken money, Ulf. So perhaps it wasn't anything to do with women after all?"

I didn't answer.

"And Pirjo in the shop said she saw you had a load of it. Money, I mean. So it's got to be worth sacrificing some of that to make sure he doesn't come back, eh, Ulf?"

"And how much would it cost?"

"No more than he offered for the opposite result. A bit less, in fact."

"Why less?"

"Because sometimes I still wake up at night with a feeling of nagging doubt. What if He does actually exist and—just like Johnny—could come back to judge the living and dead alike? Wouldn't it be better to have more good than bad deeds, so that you might get a more lenient punishment? Burn for a slightly shorter eternity at a slightly lower heat?"

"You want to blackmail me for a smaller amount

than you could get for giving me up because you think that's a *good* deed?"

Mattis sucked on his cigarette. "I said a *slightly* smaller amount. I don't want to be canonised. Five thousand."

"You're a bandit, Mattis."

"Come and see me in the morning. I'll let you have another bottle into the bargain. Drink and silence, Ulf. Proper drink, and proper silence. Things like that cost money."

He looked like a fucking goose as he waddled off down the road.

I went back in and sat down. Lea gave me a curious look.

"We have a visitor at our meeting today," Jakob Sara said, and I heard clothes rustle as the others turned round. They smiled and nodded at me. Pure warmth and friendliness. "We ask the Lord to protect him, so that he has a safe journey and soon gets back safely to where he belongs."

He bowed his head, and the congregation did the same. His prayer was muttered and indistinct, and consisted of old-fashioned words and phrases that might have meant something to the initiated. One particular word resonated with me. *Soon.*

The meeting closed with a hymn. Lea helped me to find it. I joined in. I didn't know the tune, but it was so slow that you just had to be a little late and follow the notes up and down. It was good to sing, to feel my vocal cords vibrate. Lea might have mistaken that as enthusiasm for the words, because she was smiling.

On the way out someone standing outside took me gently by the arm and directed me back into the chapel. It was Jakob Sara. He led me over to the window. I watched Lea disappear through the door. Her father waited until the last person had left before speaking.

"Did you find it beautiful?"

"In a way," I said.

"In a way," he repeated with a nod. He looked at me. "Are you thinking of taking her away from here with you?" The slow, gentle humility in his voice was gone, and the look that shot out from beneath those bushy eyebrows nailed me to the wall.

I didn't know what to say. Was he being facetious when he asked if I was thinking of running off with his daughter? Or was he not being facetious when he asked if I was thinking of running off with his daughter?

"Yes," I said.

"Yes?" One eyebrow rose.

"Yes. I'm taking her to Alta. Then back again. That's to say, she's the one taking me. She'd rather drive the car herself."

I swallowed. Hoped I hadn't caused any trouble.

That it was a sin for women to drive cars accompanied by men. Something like that.

"I know you're going to Alta," he said. "Lea sent Knut to see us. The Devil has a firm foothold in Alta. I know, I've been there."

"We'd better take some holy water and garlic." I let out a quick laugh, and immediately regretted it. His face didn't change at all, except for a spark in his eyes that vanished as quickly as it appeared, as if a sledgehammer had hit a rock somewhere in there.

"Sorry," I said. "I'm just a man passing through, you'll be rid of me *soon,* so everything can go back to the way it usually is again. The way you evidently like it."

"Are you so sure of that?"

I didn't know if he was asking if I was sure everything would return to normal, or that that was how they liked it. All I knew was that I had no great desire to continue the conversation.

"I love this country," he said, turning towards the window. "Not because it's generous or easy. As you can see, it's sparse and hard. I don't love it because it's beautiful, or admirable—it's a country like every other country. And I don't love it because it loves me. I'm a Sámi, and our rulers have treated us like disobedient children, declaring us incompetent and stripping many of us of our self-respect. I love it because it's my country. So I do what I have to to defend it. The way a father defends even his ugliest, stupidest child. Do you understand?"

I nodded to let him know that I did.

"I was twenty-two years old when I joined the resistance to fight against the Germans. They'd come here and raped my country, so what else could I do? In the middle of winter I lay out on the plateau and almost starved and froze to death. I never got to shoot any Germans—I had to stifle my bloodlust because there would have been reprisals against the local population if we'd taken action. But I felt hatred. I felt hatred, I starved, froze, and waited. And when the day finally came and the Germans disappeared, I believed that this country was mine again. But then I realised that the Russians who had arrived in the area weren't necessarily thinking of leaving again. That they could well imagine taking over my country after the Germans. We came down from the plateau to the burned-out ruins, and I found my family in a *lavvo* together with four other families. My sister told me that every night Russian soldiers would come and rape the women. So I loaded my pistol, waited, and when the first one arrived and was standing there in the opening of the *lavvo* where I had hung up a paraffin lamp, I aimed at his heart and shot. He fell like a sack. Then I cut off his head, left his military cap on, and hung the head outside the *lavvo*. None of this meant anything to me—it was like killing a cod, cutting its head off and hanging it on the racks. The next day two Russian officers came and collected the headless body of their soldier. They didn't ask any questions, and they didn't touch the head. After that no one got raped." He buttoned up his worn suit jacket. He brushed the lapel with one hand. "That was what I did, and that's what I'd do again. You protect what's yours." He looked up at me.

"It sounds like you could just have told the officers about him," I said. "And achieved the same result."

"Possibly. But I preferred to do it myself."

Jakob Sara put his hand on my shoulder.

"I can feel it's better," he said.

"Sorry?"

"Your shoulder."

Then he smiled that wilfully meek smile, raised his bushy eyebrows as if he had just thought of something that needed doing, turned round and left.

Lea was already sitting in the car when I reached the house.

I got in the passenger seat. She was wearing a simple grey coat and a red silk scarf.

"You've dressed up," I said.

"Nonsense," she said, turning the key in the ignition.

"You look nice."

"I haven't dressed up. They're only clothes. Was he being mean?"

"Your father? He was just sharing some of his wisdom with me."

Lea sighed, put the car in gear and released the clutch. We set off.

"And the talk you had with Mattis outside the prayer hall, was that about wisdom as well?"

"Oh, that," I said. "He wanted me to pay for some of his services."

"And you don't want to?"

"I don't know. I haven't decided yet."

Down by the church a figure was walking along the side of the road. As we passed I looked in the side mirror and saw her standing in the cloud of dust watching us.

"That's Anita," Lea said. She must have seen me looking in the mirror.

"Oh," I said, as neutrally as I could.

"Speaking of wisdom," she said, "Knut told me about the conversation you had with him."

"Which one?"

"He says he's going to get a girlfriend after the summer. Even if Ristiinna says no."

"Really?"

"Yes. He told me that even Futabayama the sumo legend kept on losing and losing before he started winning."

We laughed. I listened to her laughter. Bobby's had been light and bubbly, like a lively stream. Lea's was a well. No, a slowly flowing river.

In places the road curved and passed through gentle slopes, but mostly ran straight across the plateau, kilometre after kilometre. I held the strap above the door. I don't know why—you don't exactly have to hold on when you're going at sixty kilometres an hour along a flat, straight road. I've always done it, that's all. Holding the strap until my arm goes numb. I've seen other people do the same. Maybe people do have something in common after all, a desire to hold onto something solid.

Sometimes we could see the sea, at other times the road ran between hills and low, rocky knolls. The landscape lacked the striking drama of Lofoten or the beauty of Vestmark, but it had something else. A silent emptiness, a reticent relentlessness. Even the greenery of summer held a promise of harder, colder times that would try to pull you down, and which would win in the end. We encountered very few other vehicles, and saw no people or animals. Every so often there was a house or cabin, which raised the question: why? Why here, of all places?

After two and a half hours the houses began to appear more regularly, and suddenly we passed a sign at the side of the road that said "Alta."

We were—to judge by the sign—in a city.

When we came to some crossroads—the shops, schools and public buildings that surrounded it all adorned with the town's coat of arms, a white arrowhead—it turned out that the city didn't just have one centre, but three. Each of them was like a very small community of its own, but all same: who would have guessed that Alta was a miniature Los Angeles?

"When I was little, I was convinced that the world ended here in Alta," Lea said.

I wasn't sure that it didn't. According to my estimation, we were now even further north.

We parked—not a huge problem—and I managed to buy the things I wanted before the shops shut. Underwear, boots, a raincoat, cigarettes, soap and shaving equipment. Afterwards we went to a branch of Kaffistova for dinner. With the taste of fresh cod still in my mind, I searched in vain for fish on the menu. Lea shook her head with a smile.

"Up here we don't eat fish when we go out," she said. "When you're out, you want something fancy."

We ordered meatballs.

"When I was growing up, this was the time of day I liked least," I said, looking out at the deserted street.

Even the urban landscape had something oddly desolate and relentless about it: here too you had a nagging sense that nature was in control, that human beings were tiny and impotent. "Saturday after closing time, before evening fell. It was like the no man's land of the week. Sitting there with the feeling that everyone else had been invited to a party or something that was about to start. Something everyone else knew about. While you yourself didn't even have any other loser friends you could pester. It got better after the news at seven o'clock, then there was something on television and you had stuff to take your mind off it."

"We didn't have parties or television," Lea said. "But there were always people around. As a rule they wouldn't even knock; they just came in and sat in the living room and started talking. Or they just sat there quietly and listened. Father did most of the talking, of course. But Mother made the decisions. When we were at home, she was the one who decided when Father needed to calm down and give other people a chance, and when they had to go home. And we were allowed to stay up and listen to the grown-ups. It was so safe, so good. Once I remember Father crying because Alfred, a poor drunk, had finally found Jesus. When he discovered a year later that Alfred had died of an overdose down in Oslo, he drove four thousand kilometres to pick up the coffin and bring it back here so he could have a decent burial. You asked me what I believe in . . ."

"Yes?"

"That's what I believe in. People's capacity for goodness."

After dinner we went outside. It had clouded over, creating a dusk of sorts. Music was streaming from the open door of one of the kiosks advertising hot-dogs, French fries and soft ice cream. Cliff Richard. "Congratulations."

We went in. There was a couple sitting at one of the four tables. They were both smoking, and looked at us with visible disinterest. I ordered two large ice creams with chocolate sprinkles. For some reason, the white ice cream that oozed out of the machine and curled neatly into the cones made me think of a bridal veil. I took the cones over to Lea, who was standing by the jukebox.

"Look," she said. "Isn't that . . . ?"

I read the label behind the glass. Inserted a fifty-øre coin and pressed the button.

Monica Zetterlund's cool but sensual voice crept out. As did the smoking couple. Lea leaned against the jukebox; it looked as though she was soaking up every word, every note. Eyes half closed. Hips sway-ing almost imperceptibly from side to side, making the hem of her skirt move. When the song was over, she put another fifty øre in and played it again. And then again. Then we went out into the summer's evening.

Music was coming from behind the trees in the park. We automatically walked towards the sound. There was a queue of young people in front of a ticket booth. Happy, noisy, dressed in light, bright summer clothes. I recognised the poster on the ticket booth from the telephone pole in Kåsund.

"Shall we . . . ?"

"I can't," she smiled. "We don't dance."

"We don't have to dance."

"A Christian doesn't go to places like that either."

We sat down on one of the benches under the trees.

"When you say Christian . . ." I began.

"I mean Læstadian, yes. I know it can all seem a bit odd to an outsider, but we stick to the old Bible translations. We don't believe that the contents of the faith can be changed."

"But the idea of burning in hell was only read into the Bible in the Middle Ages, so that's a fairly modern invention too. Shouldn't you reject that as well?"

She sighed. "Reason lives in the head, and faith in the heart. They're not always good neighbours."

"But dancing lives in the heart too. When you were swaying in time to the music on the jukebox, did that mean you were on the verge of sinning?"

"Maybe," she smiled. "But there are probably worse things."

"Such as?"

"Well. Such as socialising with Pentecostalists, for instance."

"Is that *worse*?"

"I've got a cousin in Tromsø who sneaked out to go to a meeting of the local Pentecostalist group. When her father realised that she'd been out, she lied and said she'd been to a disco."

We both laughed.

It had got slightly darker. It was time to drive back. Even so, we remained seated.

"What do they feel when they're walking through Stockholm?" she asked.

"Everything," I replied, lighting a cigarette. "They're in love. That's why they see, hear, smell everything."

"Is that what people do when they're in love?"

"You've never experienced it?"

"I've never been in love," she said.

"Really? Why not?"

"I don't know. Obsessed, yes. But if being in love is like they say it is, then never."

"So you used to be an ice princess, then? The girl all the boys wanted, but never dared talk to."

"Me?" She laughed. "I hardly think so."

She put her hand in front of her mouth, but removed

it just as quickly. It's possible that it was unconscious, because I had trouble believing that such a beautiful woman could have a complex about a tiny scar on her top lip.

"What about you, Ulf?" She used my false name without a trace of irony.

"Loads of times."

"Good for you."

"Oh, I don't know about that."

"Why not?"

I shrugged. "It takes its toll. But I've gotten very good at handling rejection."

"Rubbish," she said.

I grinned and inhaled. "I would have been one of those boys, you know."

"Which boys?"

I knew there was no need for me to answer: her blushes revealed that she knew what I meant. I was actually a bit surprised: she didn't seem the blushing type.

I was just about to reply anyway when I was interrupted by a sharp voice:

"What the hell are you doing here?"

I turned round. They were standing behind the bench, ten metres away. Three of them. They each had a bottle in their hands. Mattis's bottles. It wasn't easy to know which of us the question was aimed at, but even in the murky light I could see and hear who had asked it: Ove. The brother-in-law with inheritance rights.

"With that . . . that . . . southerner."

The slurring in his voice made clear that he had sampled the contents of the bottle, but I suspected that wasn't wholly responsible for his failure to find a more cutting insult.

Lea sprang up and hurried towards him, putting a hand on his arm. "Ove, don't—"

"Hey, you! Southerner! Look at me! You thought you were going to get to fuck her now, did you? Now that my brother's in his grave and she's a widow. But they're not allowed to, did you know that? They're not allowed to fuck, not even then! Not until they're married again! Ha ha!" He brushed her aside before raising the bottle in a wide arc and setting it to his lips.

"Mind you, it might work with this one . . ." Alcohol and saliva sprayed from his mouth. "Because this one's a whore!" He stared at me, wild-eyed. "A whore!" he repeated when I didn't react. Not that I didn't know that calling a woman a whore is an internationally recognised signal to stand up and plant a fist in the speaker's face. But I remained seated.

"What is it, southerner? Are you a coward, as well as a cunt-thief?" He laughed, evidently pleased with himself for finally finding the right words.

"Ove . . ." Lea tried, but he shoved her away with

his drinking hand. It might not have been intentional, but the bottle caught her on the forehead. *Might* not. I stood up.

He grinned. Held the bottle out to the friends standing in the semi-darkness under a tree, came towards me with his fists raised in front of him. Legs apart, with quick, nimble steps, until he got himself into position, head slightly tilted behind his fists, with a look in his eyes that was suddenly clear and focused. As for me, I hadn't done much fighting since I left primary school. Correction. I hadn't done any fighting since primary school.

The first punch hit me on the nose, and I was blinded by the tears that instantly filled my eyes. The second one hit my jaw. I felt something come loose, and then the metallic taste of blood. I spat out a tooth and threw a wild punch at the air. His third blow hit me on the nose again. I don't know what it sounded like to them, but to me the crunch sounded like a car being crushed.

I punched another hole in the summer night. His next blow hit me in the chest as I tumbled forward and wrapped my arms round him. I tried to pin his arms down so they couldn't do any more damage, but he got his left hand free and hit me repeatedly on the ear and temple. There was a banging, squeaking sound, and it felt as if something cracked. I gnashed my teeth like a dog, got hold of something, an ear, and bit as hard as I could.

"Fuck!" he yelled, and yanked both arms free and locked my head under his right arm. I was struck by a pungent smell of sweat and adrenalin. I'd smelled it before. On men who had suddenly been confronted with the fact that they owed the Fisherman money, and didn't know what was going to happen.

"If you touch her"—I whispered into the remnants of his ear, hearing the words gurgle with my own blood—"I'll kill you."

He laughed. "And what about you, southerner? What if I knock out the rest of your lovely white teeth?"

"Go ahead," I panted. "But if you touch her . . ."

"With this?"

The only positive thing I can say about the knife he was holding in his free hand is that it was smaller than Knut's.

"You haven't got the nerve," I groaned.

He put the point of the knife to my cheek. "No?"

"Come on then, you fucking"—I couldn't work out where my sudden lisp had come from until I felt the cold steel against my tongue and realised that he'd stuck the knife right through my cheek—"inbreed," I managed to say, with some effort, seeing as it's a word that requires a certain amount of tongue gymnastics.

"What did you say, dickhead?"

I felt the knife being twisted.

"Your brother's your father," I lisped. "That's why you're so thick and ugly."

The knife was suddenly pulled out.

I knew what was coming. I knew it was going to end here. And that I'd pretty much demanded it, as good as begged for it. A man with the violent genes he had inherited didn't have any choice but to stick the knife into me.

So why did I do it? Fucked if I know. Fucked if I know what calculations go on inside our heads, the way we add and subtract in the hope of getting a positive result. I just know that fragments of that sort of calculation must have fluttered through my sleep-deprived, sun- and alcohol-addled brain, where the positive result was that a man has to spend a hell of a long time in prison for first-degree murder, and in that time a woman like Lea could get a long way away, or at least could if she had the sense to keep hold of some of the money she knew where to find. Another plus: by the time Ove was released, Knut Haguroyama would have grown up enough to protect them both. On the negative side was my own life. Which, considering the probable extent and quality of the time remaining to me, wasn't worth much. Yep, even I could do the math.

I closed my eyes. Felt the warmth of the blood running down my cheek and under my collar.

Waited.

Nothing happened.

"You *know* I'll do it," a voice said.

The grip round my head loosened.

I took two steps back. Opened my eyes again.

Ove had raised his hands and dropped the knife. Right in front of him stood Lea. I recognised the pistol she was holding, aimed at his forehead.

"Get lost," she said.

Ove Eliassen's Adam's apple bobbed up and down. "Lea . . ."

"Now!"

He leaned over to pick up the knife.

"I think you've lost that," she snarled.

He held his palms up towards her and backed away into the darkness, empty-handed. We heard angry cursing, bottles being swigged from and branches rustling as they disappeared between the trees.

"Here you are," Lea said, handing me the pistol. "It was on the bench."

"Must have slipped out," I said, and tucked it back under my waistband. I swallowed the blood from my cheek, felt my pulse hammer frantically in my temples, and noticed that I couldn't hear much from one ear.

"I saw you take it out before you stood up, Ulf."

She closed one eye. The family habit. "That hole in your cheek needs sewing up. Come on, I've got a needle and thread in the car."

I don't remember much of the journey back. Well, I remember us driving down to the Alta River, where we sat on the bank while she washed my wounds and I listened to the sound of the water and gazed at the scree, which looked like sugar piled up against the steep, pale cliff faces on either side. And I remember thinking that I had seen more sky in these days and nights than I had done in my whole life before coming here.

She felt my nose gently and concluded that it wasn't broken. Then she sewed my cheek while she talked to me in Sámi and sang something that was supposed to be a *joik* about getting better. *Joik* and the sound of the river. And I remember that I felt a bit sick, but that she waved the midges away and stroked my brow more than was strictly necessary to keep my hair away from the wound. When I asked why she had needle, thread and antiseptic in the car, and if her family was particularly prone to accidents when they were out, she shook her head.

"Not when we're out, no. A domestic accident."

"A domestic accident?"

"Yes. Called Hugo. Used to fight and was full of drink. The only thing to do was flee the house and patch up any injuries."

"You used to sew yourself?"

"And Knut."

"He hit *Knut*?"

"Where do you think he got those stitches on his forehead?"

"You sewed him back together? Here in the car?"

"It was earlier in the summer. Hugo was drunk, and it was the usual thing. He said I was looking at him with that reproachful look in my eyes, and that he wouldn't have touched me that night if only I'd had the sense to show him a bit of respect and not just ignored him. After all, I was only a girl at the time, and he was an Eliassen who had just come home from sea with a huge catch. I didn't reply, but even so he got even angrier and eventually stood up to fight. I knew how to defend myself, but at that moment Knut came in. So Hugo picked up the bottle and struck out. Hit Knut on the forehead and he collapsed in a heap, so I carried him out to the car. When I got back home Hugo had calmed down. But Knut was in bed for a week, all dizzy and nauseous. A doctor came all the way from Alta to look at him. Hugo told the doctor and everyone else that Knut had fallen down the stairs. And I . . . I didn't say anything to anyone, and I kept telling Knut that it was sure to be a one-off."

I had misunderstood. Misunderstood when Knut said his mum had told him he didn't have to worry about his dad.

"No one knew anything," she said. "Until one evening when the usual gang of drinkers was round at Ove's and someone asked what *really* happened, and Hugo told them all about his disrespectful wife and brat, and how he'd put them in their place. So the whole village knew. And then Hugo went off to sea."

"So that was what the preacher meant when he said Hugo had tried to run away from deeds he hadn't atoned for?"

"That, and everything else," she said. "Your temple's bleeding."

She took off her red silk scarf and tied it round my head.

I don't remember anything after that for quite some time. When I came to, I was curled up on the back seat of the car, and she was telling me we'd arrived. I'd probably got a bit of a concussion, she said, that was why I was so sleepy. She said it would be best if she accompanied me back to the cabin.

I walked off ahead of her and sat down on a rock when I was out of sight of the village. The light and stillness. Like the moment just before a storm. Or after a storm, a storm that had wiped out all life. Patches of mist were creeping down the green sides of the hills, like spirits in white sheets, swallowing up the small, stunted mountain birches, and as they reappeared from the mist they looked bewitched.

Then she came. Swaying, sort of, also bewitched.

"Out for a walk?" she asked with a smile. "Perhaps we're going the same way?"

Secret hiding.

My ear had started to whistle and peep, and I felt giddy, so Lea held on to me just to be on the safe side. The walk went remarkably quickly, possibly because I seemed to be drifting in and out of consciousness. Once I was finally back in the cabin I had a strange feeling of having come home, an inbuilt security and peace that I'd never felt in any of the far too many places I had lived in Oslo.

"You can sleep now," she said, feeling my forehead. "Take things easy tomorrow. And don't drink anything except water. Promise?"

"Where are you going?" I asked when she moved from the edge of the bed.

"Home, of course."

"Are you in a hurry? Knut's with his grandpa."

"Well, not too much of a hurry. I just think you ought to lie completely quiet and not talk or worry."

"I agree. But can't you lie here quietly with me? Just for a little while."

I shut my eyes. Heard her calm breathing. Imagined I could hear her weighing things up.

"I'm not dangerous," I said. "I'm not a Pentecostalist."

She laughed softly. "Just a little while, then."

I moved closer to the wall, and she squeezed in beside me on the narrow bunk.

"I'll go when you fall asleep," she said. "Knut will be home early."

I lay there, feeling myself half out of it and yet absolutely present, as my senses took in everything: the heat and pulse of her body, the scent filtering out of the neckline of her blouse, the smell of soap from her hair, the hand and arm she had placed between us so our bodies weren't in direct contact.

When I woke up I had a feeling that it was night. Something to do with the stillness. Even when the midnight sun was at its zenith, it was as if nature was resting, as if its heartbeat had slowed down. Lea's face had slipped into the crook of my neck; I could feel her nose and her even breathing against my skin. I ought to wake her, tell her it was time to go if she wanted to make sure she was home when Knut got back. Of course I wanted her to be there, so he didn't get worried. But I also wanted her to stay, at least for a few more seconds. So I didn't move, just lay there and reflected. Feeling that I was alive. As if her body was giving mine life. There was a distant rumble. And I felt her eyelashes flutter against my skin and realised she was awake.

"What was that?" she whispered.

"Thunder," I said. "Nothing to worry about, it's a long way away."

"There's never any thunder here," she said. "It's too cold."

"Maybe there's warmer weather from the south."

"Maybe. I had such bad dreams."

"What about?"

"That he's on his way. That he's coming to kill us."

"The man from Oslo? Or Ove?"

"I don't know. It slipped away from me."

We lay there listening for more thunder. None came.

"Ulf?"

"Yes?"

"Have you ever been to Stockholm?"

"Yes."

"Is it nice?"

"It's very nice in summer."

She raised herself up on one arm and looked down at me. "Jon," she said. "Leo."

I nodded. "Did the man from Oslo say that too?"

She shook her head. "I saw the tag on your necklace while you were sleeping. 'Jon Hansen, born 24 July.' I'm Libra. You're fire and I'm air."

"I'm going to burn and you're going to heaven."

She smiled. "Is that the first thing you think of?"

"No."

"What's the first thing, then?"

Her face was so close, her eyes so dark and intense.

I didn't know I was going to kiss her until I did. I'm not even sure if I was the one who did, or if it was her. But afterwards I wrapped my arms round her, pulled her to me and held her tight, feeling her body, like a pair of bellows as the air hissed out between her teeth.

"No!" she groaned. "You mustn't!"

"Lea . . ."

"No! We . . . I can't. Let me go!"

I let go of her.

She struggled out of bed. Stood there breathless in the middle of the floor, staring at me fiercely.

"I thought . . ." I said. "Sorry, I didn't mean . . ."

"Shhh," she said quietly. "That didn't happen. And it won't happen again. Never. Do you understand?"

"No."

She let out her breath in a long, trembling groan.

"I'm married, Ulf."

"Married? You're a widow."

"You don't get it. I'm not just married to him. I'm married to . . . to everything. Everything up here. You and I belong to two different worlds. You make a living from drugs, I'm a sexton, a believer. I don't know what you live for, but that's what I live for, that and my son. Nothing else matters, and I'm not going to let a . . . a stupid, irresponsible dream ruin it. I can't afford to, Ulf. Do you understand?"

"But I've already said I've got money. Look behind the plank next to the cupboard there, there's—"

"No, no, no!" She clapped her hands to her ears. "I don't want to hear, and I don't want any money! I want what I've got, nothing else. We can't see each other again, I don't want to see you again, it's ended up . . . ended up all silly and mad and . . . and now I'm going. Don't come and see me. And I won't come and see you. Goodbye, Ulf. Have a good life."

A moment later she was out of the cabin and I had already started to doubt if any of it had actually happened. Yes, she had kissed me, the pain in my cheek wasn't lying. But then the rest of it must be true as well, the part of it when she said she never wanted to see me again. I stood up and went outside, and saw her running towards the village in the moonlight.

Of course she was running away. Who wouldn't? *I* would have done. A long time ago. But then I was the type who ran away. She couldn't afford to run away, whereas as a rule I ran because I couldn't afford to stay. What had I been thinking? That two people like us could be together? No, that isn't what I'd been thinking. Dreaming of, maybe, the way our minds conjure up images and fantasies. Time to wake up now.

There was another rumble of thunder, a bit closer this time. I looked off to the west. Off in the distance banks of lead-grey clouds towered up.

That he's on his way. That he's coming to kill us.

I went back inside the cabin and leaned my forehead against the wall. I believed in dreams about as much as I believed in gods. I was more inclined to believe in a junkie's love of drugs than in people's love for one another. But I did believe in death. That was a promise I knew would be kept. I believed in a nine-millimetre bullet at a thousand kilometres an hour. And that life was the time between the moment when it left the barrel of the pistol and when it tore through your brain.

I pulled the rope out from beneath the bed and tied it round the door handle. Knotted the other end to the heavy bed-frame that was nailed to the wall so the door couldn't open outwards. I pulled it tighter. There. Then I lay down and stared at the planks of the bunk above me.

CHAPTER 13

I t was in Stockholm. A long, long time ago, before everything. I was eighteen years old, and had caught the train from Oslo. I walked around the streets of Södermalm alone. Waded through the grass on Djurgården, dangled my legs off a jetty while I looked across at the Royal Palace and knew that I would never swap what they had for the freedom I had. Then I got dressed up as best I could with the little I had, and went to the Royal Dramatic Theatre, because I was in love with a Norwegian girl who was playing Solveig in *Peer Gynt*.

She was three years older than me, but I had talked to her at a party. That must have been why I was there.

Mostly because of that. She was good in the play; she could speak Swedish like a native, or at least that's how it sounded to me. And she was attractive and unobtainable. All the same, during the course of the performance my infatuation withered away. Maybe because she couldn't compete with the day I'd had, with Stockholm. Maybe it was just that I was eighteen and had already fallen for the red-haired girl in the row in front of me.

The next day I bought some hash at Sergels torg. I walked down to Kungsträdgården, where I saw the red-haired girl again. I asked if she had enjoyed the play, but she just shrugged her shoulders and showed me how to roll a Swedish joint. She was twenty, came from Östersund, and had a little flat at Odenplan. Next door was a reasonable restaurant called Tranan, where we ate fried herring and mashed potato and drank medium-strength lager.

It turned out that she wasn't the girl I'd seen in the row in front of me after all; she'd never been to the Royal Dramatic Theatre. I stayed with her for three days. She went to work while I just wandered about breathing in the summer and the city. On the way home I sat looking out of the window, thinking about what I'd said about going back. And thought, for the first time, the most depressing thought of all: that there was no going back. That now becomes then, now becomes then in an endless fucking sequence, and there's no reverse gear on this vehicle we call life.

I woke up again.

There was something scraping at the door. I twisted over in bed and saw the door handle move up and down.

She'd changed her mind. She'd come back.

"Lea?" My heart was pounding wildly with joy, and I threw off the covers and swung my feet onto the floor.

No answer.

It wasn't Lea.

It was a man. A strong, angry man. Because the force he was using on the door handle was making the joints of the bed-frame creak.

I grabbed the rifle that was leaning against the wall and aimed it at the door.

"Who's there? What do you want?"

Still no answer. But what were they going to say? That they'd come to fix me, so could I please unlock the door? The rope quivered like a piano wire, and the door was now open a crack. Big enough to stick the barrel of a revolver through . . .

"Answer, or I'll shoot!"

It sounded like the planks of the bed were screaming in pain as the big nails were pulled out of the frame, millimetre by millimetre. And then I heard a click out-side, like a revolver being loaded.

I fired. Fired. Fired. And fired. Three bullets in the magazine and one in the chamber.

Afterwards the silence was even more oppressive.

I held my breath.

Fuck! The scraping sound was still there. There was a crash as the door handle was pulled right through the door and disappeared. Then a loud, plaintive bel-low and that same clicking sound. Which I finally recognised.

I got the pistol out from under the pillow, loosened the rope and opened the door.

The buck hadn't got far. I saw it lying on the heather twenty metres from the cabin, on the side facing the village. As if it were instinctively seeking people rather than the woods.

I went over to it.

It lay there immobile, only moving its head. The door handle was still caught in its antlers. Rubbing. It had been rubbing its horns against the door of the cabin and caught them on the handle.

It lay with its head on the ground and looked at me. I knew there wasn't really any plea in its eyes, that I was just reading that into them. I raised the pistol. Saw the movement reflected in its wet eyeballs.

What had Anita said? *You're going to shoot the*

reflection. The lone buck, who had escaped from his flock and found this hiding place, yet had still reached the end of his days—was that me?

I couldn't bring myself to fire. Of course I couldn't.

I closed my eyes. Hard. Thought about what came afterwards. About what didn't come afterwards. No more tears, no more fear, no regret, blame, thirst, longing, sense of loss, of wasting all the chances you'd been given.

I fired. Twice.

Then I walked back to the cabin.

Lay down on the bed. Kiss and death. Kiss and death.

I woke up a couple of hours later with a headache, a rushing sound in my ear, and a feeling that that was that. Gravity was pulling at my body, draining all light and hope. But I hadn't yet been dragged down so far that I couldn't pull myself out, if I was quick and grabbed onto a lifebuoy. There was only one way out, and when I sank again, the darkness would be even blacker, last even longer. But I needed that way out now.

In the absence of Prince Valium I grabbed the only lifebuoy I had. I opened the bottle of drink.

CHAPTER 14

Perhaps the drink washed the worst of the darkness away, but it couldn't wash Lea from my heart and mind. If I hadn't realised before, I knew it now. I was stupidly, hopelessly and helplessly in love. Again.

But it was different this time. There was no one in the row in front of me that I'd rather have. Just her. I wanted this inordinately Christian woman with her kid, the scar on her lip and the recently drowned husband. Lea. The girl with the raven-black hair, a blue shimmer in her eyes, and a sway in her walk. Who talked slowly, thoughtfully, without unnecessary elaboration. The woman who saw you as you were, and accepted it. Accepted *me*. That alone . . .

I turned towards the wall.

And she wanted me. Even if she had said that she never wanted to see me again, I knew she wanted me. Why else would she have kissed me? She had kissed me, and she wouldn't have done that unless she wanted to, and nothing had happened after that moment until she suddenly ran off. So unless she thought I was such a bad kisser that she'd dumped me there and then, it was simply a matter of getting her to understand that I was a man she could count on. One who'd look after her and Knut. That she'd got me wrong. That *I* had got myself wrong. I didn't want to run away, not this time. Because I had it in me, I just hadn't had a chance to prove it yet. Creating a home. But now that I thought about it, I liked the idea. Liked the idea of solidity, predictability. Yes, even uniformity and monotony. I had always looked for those things, after all. I just hadn't found them. Until now.

I laughed at myself. Couldn't help it. Because there I lay, under sentence of death, drunk, a failed contract killer, planning a long and happy life together with a woman who, the last time I talked to her, had told me in no uncertain terms that I was the last person she wanted to see again.

Then, when I turned back towards the room again and saw that the bottle on the chair in front of me was empty, I knew that one of two things was bound to happen.

I had to see her. Or I had to have more drink.

Before I slipped off into sleep again I heard a distant howl that rose and sank. They were back. They could smell death and decay, and they would soon be here.

Things were getting desperate.

I got up early. The towers of cloud were still off to the west, but they hadn't come any closer, and, if anything, seemed to have pulled back slightly. And I hadn't heard any more thunder either.

I washed in the stream. Removed the red silk scarf that was still tied round my head and bathed the wound to my temple. I put on my new underwear, new shirt. Shaved. I was about to rinse the silk scarf when I noticed it still held a little of her scent. I tied it round my neck instead. Muttered the words I was thinking of saying, words I must have changed eight times in the past hour, but I still knew them by heart. They weren't supposed to sound elaborate, just honest. And I ended with the words: "Lea, I love you." Hell, of course it had to end with that. Here I am, and I love you. Throw me out of the door if you must, if you can. But here I stand, holding out my hand to you, and in it lies my beating heart. I rinsed the razor and brushed my teeth, just in case she might want to kiss me again.

Then I started to walk down towards the village.

A swarm of flies rose up from the corpse of the reindeer as I passed. Oddly, it looked as though it had got bigger. There was a stench coming from the animal that I hadn't noticed until now, even though it was only twenty paces from the cabin. Presumably it had been swept away by the steady west wind. One of its eyes was missing. A bird of prey, probably. But it didn't look as though a wolf or any other large animal had been at it. Not yet.

I walked on. Quickly and firmly. Past the village, down to the jetty. Before I went to see Lea, I had to sort a couple of things out.

I pulled the pistol from my waistband, took a run-up of a couple of steps, and threw it as far out to sea as I could. Then I went to Pirjo's shop. I bought a tin of reindeer meatballs, just for the sake of it, and asked where Mattis lived. After trying in vain to tell me in Finnish three times, she led me outside and pointed to a house a couple of pistol throws further up the road.

Mattis opened up after I had rung the doorbell three times and was about to walk away.

"I thought I heard someone out here," he said. His hair was sticking in all directions, and he was wearing a wool sweater that was full of holes, and underpants and thick woollen socks. "The door's unlocked, so what are you doing standing here?"

"Didn't you hear the doorbell?"

He looked with interest at the object I was pointing at.

"Look at that, I've got a doorbell," he declared. "Doesn't seem like it works, though. Come in."

Mattis evidently lived in a house with no furniture.

"You live here?" I asked. My voice echoed off the walls.

"As little as possible," he said. "But this is my address."

"So who's your interior designer?"

"I inherited the house from Sivert. Someone else inherited the furniture."

"Sivert was a relative?"

"Don't know. Maybe. Actually, I suppose we had a few similarities. He probably thought we were related."

I laughed. Mattis looked at me blankly, pulled on some trousers and sat down on the floor. Crossed his legs.

I did the same.

"Forgive me asking, but what happened to your cheek?"

"I ran into a branch," I said, taking the money out of my jacket pocket.

He counted it. Grinned and stuffed it in his own pocket. "Silence," he said. "And drink, nice and cold from the cellar. What sort do you want?"

"Is there more than one?"

"No." The same grin. "Does this mean you're thinking of staying in Kåsund, Ulf?"

"Maybe."

"You're safe here now, so why go anywhere else? You'll be staying up at the cabin?"

"Where else?"

"Well ..." His grin looked as though it had been painted onto his face. "You've got to know a couple of the women here in the village. You might perchance feel like warming up a bit now that autumn's on its way."

I toyed with the idea of landing a fist right on his brown teeth. Where the hell had he got that from? I forced a smile: "Has your cousin been telling you stories, now?"

"Cousin?"

"Konrad. Kåre. Kornelius."

"He's not my cousin."

"He said he was." I tried to unfold my legs again.

"Did he?" Mattis raised an eyebrow and scratched his bushy hair. "Bloody hell, that would mean ... Hey, where are you going?"

"Away from here."

"But you haven't got your drink yet."

"I'll manage without."

"Will you?" he called after me.

212

I walked between the gravestones up to the church.

The door was ajar, so I slipped in.

She was standing by the altar with her back to me, arranging some flowers in a vase. I inhaled, trying to keep my breathing calm, but my heart was already out of control. I walked up to her with heavy strides. Even so, she jumped when I cleared my throat.

She spun round. The two steps leading up to the altar meant she was looking down at me. Her eyes were red, narrow slits under the swollen lids. I thought my heart must be visible from the outside, that it was about to start hammering dents in my chest.

"What do you want?" Her whispered voice sounded husky from crying.

It was gone.

Everything I had planned to say was gone, forgotten.

All that was left was the last sentence.

So I said it.

"Lea, I love you."

I saw her blink, as if horrified.

Encouraged by the fact that she hadn't immediately thrown me out, I went on: "I want you and Knut to come with me. To a place where no one can find us. A big city. One with an archipelago and mashed potato and medium-strength lager. We can fish and go to the

213

theatre. And afterwards we can walk slowly home to our flat on Strandvägen. I can't afford a big flat if it has to be there, because it's an expensive street. But the flat would be ours."

She whispered something as tears filled her already red eyes.

"What?" I took a step forward, but stopped when she raised her hands. She was holding a bouquet of withered flowers up protectively in front of her. She repeated herself, louder this time:

"Is that what you said to Anita as well?"

It was as if someone had tipped a bucket of water from the Barents Sea over me.

Lea shook her head. "She came here. To give me her condolences about Hugo, she said. And she had seen you and me in my car, so she wondered if I knew where you were. Seeing as you'd promised to come back."

"Lea, I . . ."

"No need, Ulf. Just get out of here."

"No! You know I needed somewhere to hide. Johnny was here looking for me. Anita offered to let me stay, and I had nowhere else to go."

I thought I could detect a tiny hint of doubt in her voice. "So you didn't touch her?"

I wanted to deny it, but it was as if my jaw muscles were paralysed, and my mouth just gaped open. Knut had been right: I'm no good at lying either.

"I ... I might have touched her, maybe. But it didn't mean anything."

"No?" Lea sniffed, and wiped away a tear with the back of her hand. "Maybe it's for the best, Ulf. I couldn't have gone anywhere with you anyway, but now at least I won't have to wonder about what might have been."

She lowered her head, turned and walked towards the sacristy. No long-winded farewell.

I wanted to run after her. Stop her. Explain. Plead. Force her. But it was as if all my energy, all my will-power had drained away.

And as the sound of the door slamming behind her echoed around the rafters, I knew that was the last time I would see Lea.

I tumbled out into the daylight. Stood there on the church steps, staring out with stinging eyes at the ser-ried ranks of gravestones.

The darkness came. I fell. The hole sucked me in, down, and not even all the drink in the world would stop it.

But of course even if it doesn't do anything to help, drink is still drink. And when I knocked on Mat-tis's door and went in, he had already put two bottles on the kitchen worktop.

"I thought you'd come back," he grinned.

I took the bottles and left without a word.

CHAPTER 15

How does a story end?

My grandfather was an architect. He said that a line—and a story—ends where it began. And vice versa.

He designed churches. Because he was good at it, he said, not because he believed in the existence of any gods. It was a way of making a living. But he said he wished he believed in the God they paid him to build churches for. That might have made the job feel more meaningful.

"I ought to design hospitals in Uganda," he said. "It could be planned in five days, and built in ten, and it would save lives. Instead I sit for months designing monuments for a superstition that doesn't save anyone."

Places of refuge, that's what he called his churches. Places of refuge from anxiety about death. Places of refuge for people's incurable hope of eternal life.

"It would have been cheaper to give people a security blanket and a teddy bear to comfort them," he said. "But it's probably better that I design churches that people can bear to look at, rather than let any of the other idiots get the job. They're littering the country with those monstrosities they call churches these days."

We were sitting in the stench of the old people's home, my rich uncle, my cousin and me, but neither of the other two was listening. Basse was just repeating things he'd said a hundred times before. They nodded, murmured in agreement, and kept glancing at the time. Before we went in, my uncle had said that half an hour was enough. I wanted to stay longer, but my uncle was driving. Basse had started to get a bit confused, but I enjoyed listening to him repeat what he thought about life. Possibly because it gave me a sense that some things were fixed, in spite of everything. *"You're going to die, take it like a man, lad!"* The only thing I was worried about was that one of the senior nurses with a crucifix round their neck would persuade him to surrender his soul to their god when the end was near. I suppose I thought that would be traumatic for a boy who had grown up with his grandfather's atheism. I didn't believe in life after death, but I did believe in death after life.

At any rate, that was now my innermost hope and desire.

Two days had passed since the door had slammed behind Lea.

Two days in bed in the cabin, two days in free fall down the hole, while I emptied one of the bottles of drink.

So how do we finish this story?

Dehydrated, I tumbled out of bed and staggered to the stream. I knelt down in the water and drank. Afterwards I just sat looking at my own reflection in an eddy behind some rocks.

And then I knew.

You're going to shoot the reflection.

Hell, why not? They weren't going to get me. *I* was going to get me. The line stops here. And what the hell would be so awful about that? *Son cuatro días,* as Basse used to say. Life lasts four days.

Almost ecstatic at my decision, I rushed back to the cabin.

The rifle was leaning against the wall.

It was a good decision, a decision with no consequences for the rest of the world. No one would cry for me, miss me, suffer any hardship. It was actually hard to think of anyone who was more dispensable than me. In short, it was a decision that would benefit everyone. So now all I had to do was put it into practice before I became too cowardly, before my sneaky, unreliable brain managed to come up with some desperate argument in favour of continuing this wretched existence.

I rested the butt of the rifle on the floor and put my mouth over the barrel. The steel tasted bitter and salty from the powder. To reach the trigger I had to stick the barrel so far into my throat that I almost hurt myself. I could just reach the trigger with my index finger. Come on, then. Suicide. The first time is always worst.

I twisted my shoulder and pulled the trigger.

There was a dry click.

Fuck.

I'd forgotten that the bullets were in the reindeer.

But I had more. Somewhere.

I searched through the cupboards and shelves. There weren't many places I could have put the box of cartridges. In the end I got down on my knees and looked under the bed, and there it was. I inserted the cartridges into the magazine. Yes, I know one bullet in your brain is enough, but it felt somehow safer knowing there was more ammunition in case anything went wrong. And yes, my fingers were trembling, so it took a while. But eventually I clicked the magazine into the rifle and loaded it the way Lea had taught me.

I put my mouth over the barrel again. It was wet with saliva and drool. I reached for the trigger. But the rifle seemed to have got longer. Or me shorter. Was I backing out?

No, I finally managed to put my finger on the trigger. And now I knew it was going to happen, that my brain wasn't going to stop me. That not even my brain could come up with good enough counterarguments, it too was longing for a rest, didn't want to fall, wanted a darkness that wasn't this darkness.

I took a deep breath and started to squeeze the trigger. The rushing sound in my ears took on a tinny note. Hang on, that wasn't coming from inside my head, it was outside. Bells ringing. The wind must have changed. And I couldn't deny that the sound of church bells felt fitting. I squeezed the trigger a little more, but it was still a millimetre or so off firing. I bent my knees, had to swallow more of the barrel, my thighs aching.

Church bells.

Now?

I'd noticed that weddings and funerals took place at one o'clock. Christenings and services on Sundays. And there were no religious holidays in August, as far as I was aware.

The barrel slid deeper into my throat. There. Now. The Germans.

Lea had told me that they rang the church bells so the members of the resistance would know when the Germans were coming for them.

I closed my eyes. Opened them again. Pulled the rifle out of my mouth. Stood up. I put it by the door and went over to the window facing the village. I couldn't see anyone. I picked up the binoculars. Nothing.

To be on the safe side I checked the other direction as well, towards the woods. Nothing. I raised the binoculars to check the ridge beyond the trees. And there they were.

There were four of them. Still so far away that it was impossible to see who they might be. Apart from one. And it wasn't too hard to guess who the other three were.

Mattis's body was rocking from side to side. Evidently the money I had given him wasn't enough, so he had laid claim to the other offer as well. Presumably he had charged them extra to show them the back way, so they could creep up on me with the best chance of not being seen.

They were too late. I was going to do the job for them. I had no desire to be tortured before I died. Not just because it hurt so much, but also because it wouldn't take long before I was yelling that I'd hidden the money in the wall of the cabin, and the dope under the floorboards in an empty flat. It was empty because people seemed to have reservations about moving into flats in which people had killed themselves. From that perspective, Toralf had made a financial miscalculation by shooting himself in his own flat. He should have picked somewhere where his heirs wouldn't suffer from the fall in value. A hunting cabin in the back of beyond, for instance.

I looked at the rifle leaning up against the wall. But I didn't touch it. I had plenty of time, they had to get through the trees and wouldn't be here for at least ten minutes, fifteen maybe. But that wasn't why.

The church bells. They were ringing. They were ringing for me. And she was the one pulling the ropes. My beloved was ignoring church customs, didn't care what the priest and the villagers would say, didn't care about her own life, because of course Mattis would have worked out what she was doing. She only had one thing on her mind: to warn the guy she didn't want to see again that Johnny was on his way to the cabin.

And that changed things.

Quite a lot of things.

They were approaching the trees now, and through the binoculars I could see the outlines of the other three. There was something birdlike about one of them, a thin neck sticking out of a jacket that was too big for him. Johnny. I could see something sticking up from the shoulders of the other two. Rifles. Automatic rifles, probably. The Fisherman had a container full of them down in his warehouse at the harbour.

I evaluated my chances. I could take them one at a time if they tried to storm the cabin. But they wouldn't do that. Mattis would help them to exploit the terrain, they'd creep down the stream to get close enough to the cabin to shoot it to pieces. I looked round. The only things I had to hide behind were made of wood, so I might as well stand in front of the cabin, waving. My only chance, in other words, was to shoot them before they shot me. And they'd have to come closer for me to do that. I'd have to look them in the face.

Three of them disappeared in amongst the trees. The fourth, one of the suits with a rifle, stayed behind and shouted something, I didn't hear what.

They wouldn't be able to see me from inside the forest for the next few minutes. This was my chance to escape. I could run to the village, take the Volkswagen. If I was going to do that, I had to do it now. Grab the money belt and . . .

Two dots.

They looked as though they were flying across the heather, down towards the trees.

Now I realised what the guy had shouted. And that

they had thought of everything. Dogs. Two of them. Silent. It struck me that dogs that didn't bark when they were out running must be bloody well trained. I wouldn't stand a chance, no matter how fast I ran.

This was starting to look bad. Maybe not quite as bad as three minutes ago, when I was standing there with a rifle barrel in my mouth, but the situation was completely different now. The distant, thin sound of church bells not only told me that some shady characters were on their way, but also that I now had something to lose. It was like getting stabbed with two knives at the same time, one hot, one cold, one happiness, one fear of dying. Hope is a real bastard.

I looked round.

My gaze fell on Knut's knife.

Happiness and fear of dying. Hope.

I waited until I saw the fourth man and the dogs disappear into the woods, then I grabbed the money belt from the wall, opened the door and ran outside.

The swarm of flies rose up from the buck as I knelt down beside it. I saw that the ants were at it as well now; it was as if the pelt of the bloated cadaver was alive. I glanced over my shoulder. The cabin was between me and the trees, so I'd be hidden until they reached it. But I didn't have long.

I closed my eyes and stuck the knife into the reindeer's stomach.

There was a long groan as the gas inside escaped.

Then I drew the knife down its belly. I held my breath as the guts spilled out. There was less blood than I expected. It had probably gathered at the bottom of the corpse. Or had coagulated, maybe. Or been eaten up. Because now I could see that it wasn't just the outside that was crawling with life. The flesh squirmed as yellowish white maggots ate, crawled and multiplied. Fucking hell.

I inhaled deeply. Closed my eyes, swallowed the vomit that rose in my throat, and pulled the silk scarf up over my mouth and nose. Then I stuck both hands inside the carcass and pulled out a huge slimy sack that I assumed was the stomach. I had to use the knife here and there to cut it loose. It sort of rolled out across the heather.

I stared into the darkness of the carcass. I didn't want to get inside. In just a few minutes, seconds, maybe, they would be here, but there still was no way I was getting inside that stinking soupy corpse. My body refused.

I heard one of the dogs bark once. Shit.

I thought of Lea, of her eyes, her lips as a smile slowly spread across her face, and her deep, warm voice saying: "You did it, Ulf."

I gulped. Then I held the flaps of skin open and forced my way inside the carcass.

Even if it was a big buck, and a good deal of the

innards had been removed, there wasn't much room. I needed to be completely hidden. And I had to try and seal it round me. I was sticky with various fluids, and it was so hot from the gases, the energy released by decomposition, and the collected heat of the mass of tiny insects moving about, the way it's always hot inside an anthill. I couldn't hold back the vomit any longer, and threw up time after time.

I gradually began to feel a bit better. But I was still visible from outside. How was I going to seal the opening in the gut? I tried grabbing hold of the two sides of the gap and holding the edges together, but they were so slimy they kept slipping out of my grasp.

I had bigger problems. Over the heather, bounding towards me, came two huge black dogs.

They threw themselves at the reindeer, and one stuck its head inside the carcass and barked at me. I jabbed the knife at it and the head disappeared. Then the barking started. I had to get the carcass sealed before the men arrived. The barking was getting louder, and then I heard voices as well.

"The cabin's empty!"

"There's an animal down there!"

I stuck the knife through the reindeer skin at the bottom of the opening, pulled in the skin at the top, and managed to stick the knife through that as well before I lost my grip.

I used the knife as a bobbin, two twists were enough, then the gap was sealed. Now I just had to wait and hope no one had taught the dogs to talk.

I heard steps approaching.

"Get the dogs away, Styrker. I thought you could control them."

I felt a chill run through me. Yep, that was the voice of the man who had come to my flat to kill me. Johnny was back.

"It must be the carcass," Styrker said. "It's not easy when you've got a tiny brain and plenty of instincts."

"Are you talking about the dogs or yourself?"

"Christ, what a stink," a third voice groaned. I recognised it at once: Brynhildsen from the back room, the one who was always cheating. "What's that caught on its horns? And why are the guts out here on the ground? Shouldn't we check . . . ?"

"The wolves have been at it," Mattis said. "Forgive me saying, but don't breathe in too much of the stench, it's poisonous."

"Really?" Johnny's quiet voice.

"Botulism," Mattis said. "The spores fly through the air. One spore is enough to kill a person."

Bloody hell! After all this am I going to die like that, in here, from some fucking bacteria?

"The symptoms are an unpleasant tiredness in the eyes," Mattis went on. "And your ability to express yourself vanishes. That's why we burn dead reindeer straight away. So that we can still see each other and make sensible conversation."

There was a pause, during which I could imagine Johnny staring at Mattis and trying to interpret his inscrutable half-grin.

"Styrker and Brynhildsen," Johnny said. "Turn the cabin inside out. And take those bloody dogs with you."

"He's not in there, there's no way he could be," Brynhildsen insisted.

"I know that. But if we can find the money and dope, we know he's still in the area."

I heard the dogs bark frantically as they were dragged away.

"Forgive me asking, but what happens if you don't find anything?"

"Then you might have been right after all," Johnny said.

"I *know* he was the one sailing that boat," Mattis said. "It was only fifty metres from shore, and he's an ugly southerner. We don't have people like that up here. With a decent boat and a good wind behind him, he could cover quite some distance in a day."

"And you were lying on the seashore in the middle of the night?"

"Best place to sleep in the summer."

I felt something crawling at the bottom of my shin.

Too big to be a maggot or ant. I was breathing through my mouth, not my nose. Snake or mouse? Please, let it be a mouse. A sweet, furry little mouse, even a hungry one, but not a . . .

"Really?" Johnny's voice was even lower now. "And the quickest way from the village and up to the forest is to go *round* the whole ridge? It took us over an hour. When I came up here on my own the last time I was here, it barely took me half an hour."

"Yes, but you'd have been shot if he'd been at home."

The animal—or whatever it was—was moving over my foot. I felt an almost irresistible urge to kick it off, but I knew that the slightest movement or sound would be detected.

"You know what?" Johnny sneered. "That's what I can't help wondering about."

"Oh? You might be a narrow-shouldered target, southerner, but your head's big enough."

"It's not that Jon Hansen can't shoot. It's that he hasn't got the guts to."

"Really? Well, I could have shown you a quicker route if you'd mentioned that before—"

"I did mention it, you Sámi bastard!"

"In north Norwegian."

The creature had reached my knee and was moving onto my thigh. It suddenly dawned on me that it was inside my trousers.

"Shhh!"

Had I yelped or moved?

"What was that noise?"

Total silence out there now. I held my breath. Dear God . . .

"Church bells," Mattis said. "They're burying William Svartstein today."

What if it was a lemming? I'd heard that they were nervous little fuckers, and now it was approaching the crown jewels. Without making any obvious movement, I took hold of my trouser leg and pulled it tight in my clenched hand, making the fabric cling to my thigh and blocking the creature's path.

"Well, I've had enough of this stink," Johnny said. "Let's check down by the stream. If the dogs are still confused by the smell of the reindeer, he might have hidden there."

I heard them walk off through the heather. Inside my trousers the creature pushed against the blockage in the tunnel for a while, then resigned itself to going back the way it had come. Shortly after that I heard a voice call out from the cabin: "There's nothing here, just a rifle and his suit!"

"Okay, lads, let's get back before the rain comes."

I waited for what felt like an hour, but it could have been ten minutes. Then I pulled the knife out of the reindeer skin and peered out.

The coast was clear.

I crept through the heather towards the stream. I slid into the ice-cold water, letting it pour over me, washing me clean of death, shock and decay.

Slowly, slowly, I came back to life.

CHAPTER 16

*D*ear God . . .

    I hadn't said it, but I thought it there inside the animal carcass, I thought it as loudly as if I'd stood on a street corner and shouted it. And the monsters had gone, the way they did when I was little and they were hiding under my bed, or in the toy box, or in the wardrobe.

Could it be that simple? Did you just have to pray?

I was sitting outside the cabin, smoking and looking up. The leaden grey clouds were covering the whole sky now, and had brought darkness with them. It was as if the weather were running a fever. It was oppressively muggy and warm, then the next moment icy cold when the wind gusted.

God. Salvation. Paradise. Eternal life. It was an appealing thought. Tailor-made for scared, battered hearts. So appealing that Grandfather finally gave in and abandoned his reason and staked everything on hope. "You don't say no to something that's free, you know," he told me with a wink. Like a broke sixteen-year-old sneaking into a disco with a forged ticket and a fake ID.

I packed the few things that would be coming with me. Clothes, shoes, suit, rifle and binoculars. The clouds hadn't let go of any rain yet, but it couldn't last much longer.

Johnny would be back. It was obvious that he didn't believe Mattis. And that was clearly the right thing to do when it came to Mattis. A detour round the whole ridge. Wolves. Botulism. That he'd seen me sail away. William Svartstein's funeral.

I didn't remember much of my wasted years at university, but I did remember William Blackstone, the eighteenth-century legal philosopher who occupied much the same territory as Mattis, at the crossroads of justice and faith in God. I remembered him because Grandfather had used him, Isaac Newton, Galileo Galilei and Søren Kierkegaard as examples of the fact that even the very sharpest minds are prepared to believe in the stuff and nonsense of Christianity if they think it offers a chance to escape death.

Mattis hadn't betrayed me. On the contrary, he had saved me. So who had contacted Johnny and told him I hadn't left Kåsund after all?

Another gust of wind, as if the weather wanted to tell me to get a move on. There was rumbling off to the west. Okay, okay, I was ready to leave now. It was night. If Johnny and the others hadn't already left Kåsund, they would be asleep somewhere.

I stubbed my cigarette out on the cabin wall, picked up the leather case and slung the rifle over my shoulder. I walked down the path without looking back. Only forward. And that was how it was going to be from now on. Whatever was behind me could remain exactly that.

The sky rumbled and crackled with anticipation as I stepped out onto the gravel road. It was so dark that all I could see was the shapes of the houses and the few windows that were lit up.

I didn't believe, expect or hope anything. I just wanted to call in and return the rifle and binoculars, and thank her for the loan. And for my life. And ask if she possibly felt like spending the rest of her life with me. And then leave, with or without her.

I passed the church. Anita's house. The prayer hall. And then I was standing in front of Lea's house.

A shining, crooked witch's finger suddenly pointed down at me from the sky. The house, garage and wrecked Volvo were momentarily lit up by a ghostly blueish light. Then there was a crackling prelude before the storm broke loose.

They were in the kitchen.

I saw them through the window, the light inside was on. She was leaning against the worktop, her body arched back in a stiff, unnatural posture. Ove stood with his head thrust forward, holding a knife in his hand. It was larger than the one he had used on me. He was waving it in front of her face. Threatening her. She leaned back even further, away from the knife, away from her brother-in-law. He grabbed her neck with his free hand, I saw her cry out.

I put the rifle to my shoulder. Got his head in the sights. He was standing side-on to the window, so I could hit him in the temple. But a vague idea about the refraction of light through glass was whirling about my head, and I lowered my aim slightly. Chest height. I raised my elbows, took one deep breath—there wasn't time for more—lowered my elbows again, breathed out, and slowly squeezed the trigger. I felt strangely calm. Then another finger of light tore at the sky, and I saw his head turn automatically towards the window.

Everything around me was dark again, but he was still staring at the window. At me. He had seen me.

He looked more ravaged than last time—he must have been drinking for days. Psychotic from lack of sleep, or mad with love, mad with grief for his brother, mad at being trapped in a life he didn't want. Yes, perhaps that was it, perhaps he was like me.

You're going to shoot the reflection.

So this was my fate: shooting a man, getting arrested by the police, convicted and sent to prison, where the Fisherman's men would soon appear and put a definite end to it all. Fine. I could accept that. That wasn't the problem. The problem was that I had seen his face.

I could feel my index finger start to weaken, as the spring in the trigger gained the upper hand and forced my powerless finger back. I wasn't going to manage it. I wasn't going to manage it, again.

There was another crack of thunder above me, like a voice barking an order.

Knut.

Even Futabayama kept on losing before he started to win.

I took another deep breath. I had got rid of my block. I aimed the sights straight at Ove's ugly face and fired.

The blast echoed across the rooftops. I lowered the rifle. Looked through the shattered glass. Lea was holding her hands up in front of her mouth and staring down at something. Beside her, on the white

237

wall above her head, it looked as though someone had painted a grotesque rose.

The last echo died away. The whole of Kåsund must have heard it; soon the village would be crawling with people.

I went up the steps. Knocked—I don't know why. Went in. She was still standing in the kitchen. She hadn't moved, was staring down at the body lying in a pool of blood on the floor. She didn't look up, I don't know if she even knew I was there.

"Are you okay, Lea . . . ?"

She nodded.

"Knut . . ."

"I sent him to Father's," she whispered. "I thought that if they worked out why I was ringing the church bells, they'd come here and . . ."

"Thank you," I said. "You saved my life."

I tilted my head and looked down at the dead man. He stared back with broken eyes. He was more suntanned than last time, and his face was otherwise unharmed. Just an almost innocent-looking hole in his forehead, right under his blond fringe.

"He came back," she whispered. "I *knew* he was going to come back."

That was when it struck me. That his left ear was uninjured. That there wasn't so much as a hint of a mark on it. And there should have been; the bite was only a couple of days old. Then it slowly dawned on me. When Lea said he had come back, she meant . . .

"I *knew* there was no sea or earth that could hold this devil down," she said. "No matter how deep we buried him."

It was Hugo. The twin brother. I had shot the reflection.

I shut my eyes tight. Opened them again. But nothing had changed, I hadn't dreamed it all. I had murdered her husband.

I had to clear my throat to make my voice heard:

"I thought it was Ove. It looked like he was trying to kill you."

At last she stared at me.

"Better you killed Hugo than Ove. Ove would never have dared touch me."

I nodded towards the body. "But he would?"

"He was one jab of the knife away from it."

"Because?"

"Because I told him."

"What?"

"That I want to get away from here. That I want to take Knut with me. That I never wanted to see him again."

"You didn't want to see him again, either?"

"I told him that I . . . I'm in love with someone else."

"Someone else."

"You, Ulf." She shook her head. "I can't help it. I love you."

The words trembled round the walls like a hymn. And the blue light in her eyes was so strong that I had to look away. One of her feet was in the spreading pool of blood.

I took a step towards her. Two. Put both feet in the blood. Gently put my hands round her shoulders. I wanted to check first that it was okay for me to pull her towards me. But before I figured it out she had fallen towards me and buried her face under my chin. She sobbed once, twice. I felt her warm tears trickling down under the collar of my shirt.

"Come," I said.

I ushered her into the living room, where a lightning flash lit up the room and showed me the way to the sofa. We lay down on it, close together.

"I got such a shock when he was suddenly standing there in the kitchen door," she whispered. "He said he'd got drunk on his boat with the engine running. When he woke up, he was a long way out to sea and the petrol had run out. He had oars, but the wind just kept driving the boat further out. The first few days he thought it was probably for the best. After all, we had made him think everything was his fault, that he was worthless after he hurt Knut. But then the rain came, and he survived. And then the wind changed direction. And that was when he decided it hadn't been his fault." She let out a bitter laugh. "He stood there and said he was going to sort everything out, that he'd sort me and Knut out. When I told him Knut and I were going to leave, he asked if there was someone else. So I said we would be leaving on our own, but that, yes, I did love someone else. I thought it was important for him to know that. That I was capable of loving a man. Because then he would realise that he could never get me back."

While she was talking the temperature in the room had fallen, and she huddled closer to me. So far nobody had come to see why the rifle had been fired. And as the next clap of thunder broke, I realised why. And that no one was going to come.

"Is anyone else aware he came back?" I asked.

"I don't think so," she said. "He saw some familiar landmarks this afternoon and rowed home. He tied the boat up at the jetty and came straight here."

"When was that?"

"Half an hour ago."

Half an hour ago. When everything was dark, and the thundery weather would have kept everyone indoors. No one had seen Hugo, no one knew he was alive. *Had been* alive. With the possible exception of one man who was fond of rolling about at night. To everyone else Hugo Eliassen was just a fisherman who had been claimed by the sea. One they were no longer searching for. I wished it was me. Me that they were no longer searching for. But, as Johnny had said: *The Fisherman never stops looking for his debtors until he sees the corpse.*

Another flash of lightning lit up the room. Then it was dark again. But I had seen it. Seen it perfectly clearly. Like I said, the brain is a strange and remarkable thing.

"Lea?" I said.

"Yes?" she whispered against my neck.

"I think I've got a plan."

CHAPTER 17

*S*corched-earth tactics.

That's how I thought of my plan. I would retreat the way the Germans did. And then I would disappear. Disappear completely.

The first thing we did was wrap the body in plastic bags and tie them up with rope. Then we washed the floor and walls thoroughly. Dug the bullet out from the kitchen wall. Lea tipped the wheel rims out of the wheelbarrow and pushed it into the garage, where I was waiting with the body. I loaded it onto the barrow. Stuck the rifle in underneath him. We tied a rope to the front of the wheelbarrow so Lea could help pull it. I went into the workroom and found a small pair of pliers. Then we set off.

There wasn't a single person around outside and it was still reassuringly gloomy. I reckoned it would be another three or four hours before people started to get up, but we had thrown a tarpaulin over the barrow just in case. It went easier than I had expected. When my arms were tired Lea would take a turn behind the barrow while I pulled it.

Knut had seen them pull up in a car with Oslo plates.

"He came racing in and told me there were three men and two dogs," Lea said. "He wanted to run up and warn you, but I said it was too dangerous because of the dogs. They'd pick up his scent and maybe come after him as well. So I ran to Mattis and told him he had to help me."

"To Mattis?"

"When you said he'd asked you for money for various services, I had a good idea of what those might be. He'd been paid not to contact Oslo and give you up."

"But how did you know he hadn't already done that?"

"Because it was Anita."

"Anita?"

"She didn't come to pass on her condolences. She came to find out if I had a good explanation for why I'd been sitting in a car with you. And I could see that my explanation wasn't good enough. She knows

I wouldn't just go shopping in Alta with a stranger from the south. And I know what a woman scorned is capable of . . ."

Anita. *No one makes a promise to Anita without keeping it.*

She had a stake in my soul, Johnny's phone number, and the sense to put two and two together. I had got whatever she was spreading after all.

"But you trusted Mattis?" I said.

"Yes."

"He's a liar and a blackmailer."

"And a cynical businessman who never gives you a drop more than you've paid for. But he sticks to agreements. And he also owed me a couple of favours. I asked him to lead them away from you, or at the very least to delay them, while I went up to the church to ring the bells."

I told her how Mattis had sworn blind that he'd seen me leave Kåsund by boat. And how, when they still insisted on checking the cabin, he'd led them on a long detour. Without that detour they'd probably have arrived before the wind changed and I heard the church bells.

"A strange man," I said.

"A strange man," she laughed.

It took us an hour to get to the cabin. The weather had turned noticeably colder, but the clouds were still

hanging low. I prayed it wasn't about to rain. Not yet.
I wondered if this business of praying was going to
become a habit.

As we got closer I thought I saw some shapes disappear without a sound, racing up the ridge at great
speed. The reindeer's guts had been pulled apart, and
the carcass was fully open.

They had conducted a thorough search for the
money and dope, the mattress had been torn open,
the wall cabinet pulled down, the stove opened and the
ashes dug through. The last bottle of drink lay under
the table, and the floorboards had been pulled up
and the planks lining the walls torn off. Which sug-
gested that the drugs hidden in Toralf's flat weren't
going to be safe if they ever thought to look there. But
that was fine, I wasn't thinking of going to get them. I
wasn't actually planning to have anything to do with
drugs from now on. For various reasons. Not many
reasons, really, but those I had were all very good ones.

Lea waited outside while I cut the body free of the
plastic. I put several layers of roofing felt on the bed
before heaving the corpse onto it. I took his wedding
ring off. Perhaps he'd lost weight while he was at sea,
or perhaps it had always been a bit loose. I took off
my chain with the ID dog tag and hung it round his
neck. Then I felt around in my mouth with the tip of
my tongue to check which tooth was broken, took out

the pliers and fastened them round the matching tooth in his mouth, and snapped it off at the gum. I laid the rifle on his stomach and the misshapen bullet under his head. I glanced at my watch. Time was getting on.

I covered the body with another layer of roofing felt, opened the bottle of alcohol and soaked the bed, the felt and the rest of the cabin. There was a tiny bit left. I hesitated for a moment. Then I turned the bottle upside down and watched Mattis's unholy liquor soak into the tinder-dry floorboards.

I took a match out of the box, shuddered as I heard the sulphur scrape against the side of the box and watched the flame flare up.

Now.

I dropped the match on top of the roofing felt.

I've read that bodies don't burn well. We're sixty per cent water, maybe that's why. But as I saw how quickly the tar-covered felt burned, I didn't expect there to be much meat left on the grill afterwards.

I went outside, leaving the door open so that the first flames would catch properly and really take hold.

I needn't have worried.

It was as if the flames were talking to us. First with mumbling, restrained voices, then they gradually rose in volume and wildness, until eventually they were a cacophonous roar. Even Knut would have been happy with this blaze.

As if she knew who I was thinking about, she said: "Knut always used to say that his father would burn."

"What about us?" I said. "Will we burn?"

"I don't know," she said, taking my hand. "I've tried to work it out, but the funny thing is that I don't feel anything. Hugo Eliassen. I lived under the same roof as that man for over ten years, but even so I'm not sorry, and I don't feel any sympathy for him. I'm not angry with him anymore, but I don't feel happy either. And I'm not scared. It's been a long while since I wasn't scared. Scared for Knut's sake, for my own. I was even scared for you. But do you know what the strangest thing is?"

She swallowed and stared at the cabin, which was now a single mass of flames. She looked incredibly beautiful in the red glow of the fire.

"I don't regret it. Not now, and I won't regret it later either. So if what we're doing is a mortal sin, then I'll burn, because I'm not going to ask for forgiveness. The only thing I've regretted these past few days"— she turned towards me—"is that I let you go."

The nocturnal temperature had fallen suddenly and severely; it must have been the heat from the cabin that was making my cheeks and forehead burn.

"Thank you for not giving up, Ulf." She stroked my hot cheek with her hand.

"Hmm. Not Jon?"

She leaned against me. Her lips almost touching mine. "Considering the plan, it's probably best if we carry on calling you Ulf."

"Speaking of names and plans," I said. "Would you like to marry me?"

She looked at me sharply. "You're proposing *now*? While my husband is burning to ashes right in front of us?"

"It's the practical solution," I said.

"Practical!" she snorted.

"Practical." I folded my arms. Looked up at the sky. Then at the time. "Plus the fact that I love you more than I've ever loved any woman, and that I've heard Læstadian women aren't even allowed to kiss before marriage."

A shower of sparks flew up as the roof and walls of the cabin collapsed. She pressed closer to me. Our lips met. And this time there was no doubt.

She was kissing me.

As we hurried down towards the village, the cabin was already a smoking ruin behind us. We agreed that I should hide in the church while she packed and picked up Knut from his grandparents, before fetching me in the Volkswagen.

"You don't need to pack much," I said, patting the money belt. "We can buy what we need."

She nodded. "Don't show yourself outside. I'll come in and get you."

We parted on the gravel road, right where I had met Mattis the night I arrived in Kåsund. That felt like a lifetime ago. And now, as then, I heaved the heavy church door open and went up to the altar. There I stopped and looked at the crucifix.

Did Grandfather mean what he said about not being able to turn down something that was free, and that was the only reason why he surrendered to superstition? Or was it actually the case that my prayers had been heard, that the guy on the cross had saved me? Did I owe him anything?

I took a deep breath.

Him? He was just a man carved out of fucking wood. Down by the shore there were rocks they prayed to that must work just as well.

But all the same.

Damn.

I sat down on the front pew. Thinking. And it isn't too pretentious to say that I was thinking about life and death.

After twenty minutes the door slammed hard. I swung round. It was too dark for me to see who it was. But it *wasn't* Lea; the footsteps were too heavy.

Johnny? Ove?

My heart was racing as I tried to remember why I'd tossed the pistol into the sea.

"So." The vowel was stretched out. The voice was deep and familiar. "You're having a conversation with the Lord? I presume you're asking if you're doing the right thing?"

For some reason I saw Lea's features more clearly in her father, now that he had come straight from bed. What little hair he had wasn't as neatly combed as the other times I had seen him, and his shirt was buttoned wrong. That made him less intimidating, but beyond that there was something about his tone of voice and facial expression that told me he had come in peace.

"I'm not quite a believer yet," I said. "But I'm no longer denying that I've got doubts."

"Everyone has doubts. Believers more than anyone."

"Really? You, too?"

"Of course I have doubts." Jakob Sara sat down beside me with a groan. He wasn't a heavy man, but even so the pew seemed to rock. "That's why it's called faith, not knowledge."

"Even for a preacher?"

"Especially for a preacher." He sighed. "He has to confront his own convictions every time he preaches the Word. He has to feel it, because he knows that doubt and faith will each be audible in his voice. Do I believe today? Do I believe *strongly enough* today?"

251

"Hmm. What about the times you step up to the pulpit when you don't believe strongly enough?"

He rubbed his chin. "Then you have to believe that living as a Christian is in itself good. That renunciation, not succumbing to sin, has a value for human beings even in this earthly life. On a similar theme, I've read that sportsmen find the pain and effort of training meaningful in itself, even if they never win anything. If heaven didn't actually exist, then at least we have a good, secure life as Christians, where we work, live happily, accept the possibilities God and nature give us, and look after each other. Do you know what my father—also a preacher—used to say about Læstadianism? That if you only counted the people the movement had saved from alcoholism and broken homes, that alone would justify what we do, even if we were preaching a lie." He paused for a minute. "But it's not always like that. Sometimes it costs more than it should to live according to Scripture. The way it did for Lea ... The way I, in my delusion, forced Lea to live." There was a faint tremor in his voice. "It took me many years to realise it, but no one should be forced by their father to live in a marriage like that, with a man they hate, a man who had taken them by force." He raised his head and looked at the crucifix above us. "Yes, I remain convinced that it was right according to Scripture, but sometimes salvation can have too high a price."

"Amen."

"And the pair of you, you and Lea . . ." He turned to look at me. "I saw it in the prayer hall. Two young people looking at each other in the way you and Lea did in the back row, when you thought no one else could see." He shook his head and smiled sadly. "Now of course what Scripture says about remarriage is debatable, not to mention marrying a heathen. But I've never seen Lea like this. And I've never *heard* her sound the way she did when she came to pick up Knut just now. You've made my daughter beautiful again, Ulf. I'm just saying it like it is, and it looks as if you've started to heal all the damage I did." He put a large, wrinkled hand on my knee. "And you're doing the right thing, you need to get away from Kåsund. The Eliassen family is very powerful, more powerful than me, and they'd never let you and Lea have a life here."

Now I understood. After the prayer meeting in the hall, when he asked if I was thinking of taking Lea away from there with me . . . he hadn't meant it as a threat. It had been a plea.

"Besides . . ." He patted my knee. "You're dead, aren't you, Ulf? I've had my instructions from Lea. You were a lonely, depressed soul who set fire to the hunting cabin before lying down on the bed and shooting yourself in the head with the rifle. The charred corpse will bear a metal dog tag with your name on it, and both I and Ove Eliassen will swear to the police that you were missing one of your front teeth. I shall inform whatever family you may have, explain that you had expressed a wish to be buried here, sort out the paperwork, talk to the vicar and get your remains in the ground quickly and efficiently. Any particular hymns you'd like?"

I turned to look at him. Saw one of his gold teeth flash in the half-light.

"I'll be the only person here who knows the truth," the old man said. "And even I don't know where you're going. And I don't want to know either. But I hope to see Lea and Knut again someday." He stood up with creaking knees.

I got to my feet and held my hand out to him. "Thank you."

"I should be thanking you," he said. "Because you've given me the chance to make good at least some of what I did to my daughter. The peace of God, farewell, and may all His angels go with you on your journey."

I followed him with my eyes as he left. Felt a gust of cold air as the door opened and closed again.

I waited. Looked at the time. Lea was taking longer than I had anticipated. I hoped she hadn't run into any trouble. Or changed her mind. Or . . .

I heard the stuttering sound of a forty-horsepower engine outside. The Volkswagen. I was about to head towards the door of the church when it flew open and three people came in.

"Stay where you are!" a voice roared. "This won't take long."

The man rolled quickly up between the pews. Knut was following him, but it was Lea who caught my eye. She was dressed in white. Was that her wedding dress?

Mattis stopped in front of the altar. Put on a pair of comically small glasses and leafed through some papers he pulled from the pocket of his anorak. Knut jumped up onto my back.

"There's something on my back!" I said, twisting and turning.

"Yep, *rikishi* Knut-*san* from Finnmark *ken*!" Knut squealed as he clung on tight.

Lea walked up beside me and put her hand under my arm.

"I thought it was best to get it sorted out straight away," she whispered. "Practical."

"Practical," I repeated.

"Let's get straight to the important bit," Mattis said, then cleared his throat and held the papers close to his face. "In the sight of God the Creator, and with the authority vested in me as a representative of the Norwegian judiciary, forgive me asking, but do you, Ulf Hansen, take Lea Sara to be your lawfully wedded wife?"

"Yes," I said loudly and clearly. Lea squeezed my hand.

"Will you love and honour her, be faithful to her"—he leafed through the documents—"in sickness and in health?"

"Yes."

"Now I ask you, Lea Sara, will you—?"

"Yes!"

Mattis looked up over his glasses. "What?"

"Yes, I take Ulf Hansen to be my lawfully wedded husband, and I promise to love and honour and be faithful to him until death us do part. Which won't be long unless we get a move on."

"Of course, of course," Mattis said, and looked through his papers. "Let's see, let's . . . here it is! Take each other's hands. Ah, I see you've already done that. In that case . . . right! In the sight of God—and me, as representative of the Norwegian authorities—you have promised . . . lots of things. And you have each given your hand to the other. I therefore declare you to be legally married."

Lea looked up at me. "Let go now, Knut."

Knut let go, slid down off my back and landed on the floor behind me. Then Lea kissed me quickly and turned back to Mattis again. "Thanks. Can you sign the papers?"

"Of course," Mattis said. He clicked the back of a

ballpoint pen against his chest, put his name on one of the papers and handed it to her. "That's an official document and ought to be valid wherever you go."

"Will it work as a way of getting new ID papers?" I asked.

"Your date of birth is here, here are our signatures, and your wife can confirm your identity as Ulf Hansen, so yes, it ought to be enough to get at least a temporary passport from a Norwegian embassy."

"That's all we need."

"Where are you going?"

We looked at him in silence.

"Of course," he muttered, and shook his head. "Good luck."

And that was how we came to walk out of church in the middle of the night as a married couple. I was married. And, if Grandfather was right, the first time is always the worst. Now we just had to jump in the Volkswagen and get out of Kåsund before anyone woke up and saw us. But we stopped on the steps and looked up in astonishment.

"Confetti!" I said. "That's all that was missing."

"It's snowing!" Knut cried.

Big, fluffy flakes of snow drifted slowly down from the sky and settled on Lea's black hair. She laughed out loud. Then we ran down the steps and over to the car, and got in.

Lea turned the key in the ignition, the engine started, she let out the clutch and we were on our way.

"Where are we going?" Knut asked from the back seat.

"Top secret," I said. "All I can say is that it's the capital of a country where we don't need passports to cross the border."

"What are we going there for?"

"We're going to live there. Try to get jobs. And play."

"What are we going to play?"

"A lot of things. Secret hiding, for instance. By the way, I've thought of a joke. How do you fit five elephants into a Volkswagen?"

"Five . . ." he muttered to himself. Then he leaned forward between the seats. "Tell me!"

"Two in the front and three in the back."

A moment's silence. Then he fell back into his seat and let out a loud laugh.

"Well?" I said.

"You're getting better, Ulf. But that wasn't a joke."

"No?"

"That was a riddle."

He fell asleep before we left the county of Finnmark.

It was day by the time we passed the Swedish border. The monotonous landscape slowly changed, taking on more colour and variety. The mountains were covered by a scattering of snowy powdered sugar. Lea hummed a song she'd only recently learned.

"There's a hotel just outside Östersund," I said, leafing through the gazetteer I had found in the glove compartment. "It looks nice, we can get a couple of rooms there."

"Our wedding night," she said.

"What about it?"

"That'll be tonight, won't it?"

I thought. "Yes, I suppose it will. Look, we've got loads of time, we don't need to rush anything."

"I don't know what *you* need, dear husband," she said in a low voice, checking in the mirror that Knut was still asleep. "But you know what they say about Læstadians and wedding nights."

"No."

She didn't answer. Just sat there steering our car and following the road with an inscrutable smile on her red lips. Because I think she knew what I needed. I think she knew from the moment she asked the question that night in the cabin, the one I didn't answer: what was the first thing I thought of when she said I was fire and she air. Because, as Knut would say, everyone knows the answer to that riddle.

Fire needs air to exist.

Damn, she's so beautiful.

———

So how do we end this story?

I don't know. But I'm going to stop telling it here.

Because right here is good. Maybe things will happen later that aren't quite so good. But I don't know that yet. I just know that right here and now everything is perfect, that right now I am in a place where I have always wanted to be. On my way, but already there.

I'm ready.

Daring to lose, one more time.

The descriptions of Finnmark—which is fairly unfamiliar territory even for Norwegians—are partly drawn from my own experiences of travelling and living in the area in the 1970s and early 1980s, and partly from other people's accounts of Sámi culture, including Øyvind Eggen, who has kindly given me permission to draw on his dissertation on Læstadianism.

THE BAT

Inspector Harry Hole of the Oslo Crime Squad is dispatched to Sydney to observe a murder case. Harry is free to offer assistance, but he has firm instructions to stay out of trouble. The victim is a twenty-three-year-old Norwegian woman who is a minor celebrity back home. Never one to sit on the sidelines, Harry befriends one of the lead detectives, and one of the witnesses, as he is drawn deeper into the case. Together, they discover that this is only the latest in a string of unsolved murders, and the pattern points toward a psychopath working his way across the country. As they circle closer and closer to the killer, Harry begins to fear that no one is safe, least of all those investigating the case.

Thriller

COCKROACHES

When the Norwegian ambassador to Thailand is found dead in a Bangkok brothel, Inspector Harry Hole is dispatched from Oslo to help hush up the case. But once he arrives Harry discovers that this case is about much more than one random murder. There is something else, something more pervasive, scrabbling around behind the scenes. Or, put another way, for every cockroach you see in your hotel room, there are hundreds behind the walls. Surrounded by round-the-clock traffic noise, Harry wanders the streets of Bangkok lined with go-go bars, temples, opium dens, and tourist traps, trying to piece together the story of the ambassador's death even though no one asked him to, and no one wants him to—not even Harry himself.

Thriller

THE REDEEMER

Shots ring out at a Salvation Army Christmas concert in Oslo, leaving one of the singers dead in the street. The trail will lead Inspector Harry Hole, Oslo's best investigator and worst civil servant, deep into the darkest corners of the city and, eventually, to Croatia. An assassin forged in the war-torn region has been brought to Oslo to settle an old debt. As the police circle in, the killer becomes increasingly desperate and the danger mounts for Harry and his colleagues.

Thriller

THE SNOWMAN

One night, after the first snowfall of the year, a boy named Jonas wakes up and discovers that his mother has disappeared. Only one trace of her remains: a pink scarf, his Christmas gift to her, now worn by the snowman that inexplicably appeared in their yard earlier that day. Inspector Harry Hole suspects a link between the missing woman and a suspicious letter he's received. The case deepens when a pattern emerges: over the past decade, eleven women have vanished—all on the day of the first snow.

Thriller

ALSO AVAILABLE

Headhunters
The Leopard
Phantom
Police
The Snowman

VINTAGE CRIME/BLACK LIZARD
Available wherever books are sold.
www.weeklylizard.com